Praise for Pamela Britton

"It isn't easy to write a tale that makes the reader laugh and cry, but Britton succeeds."
—*Booklist*

"What makes Britton's work stand out in the genre is her humor."
—*The Pinnacle News*

"Pamela Britton is well on her way to stardom."
—*Romantic Times BOOKclub*

"Pamela Britton writes the kind of wonderfully romantic, sexy, witty romance that readers dream of discovering when they go into a bookstore."
—Bestselling author Jayne Ann Krentz

"Passion and humor are a potent combination, and author Pamela Britton comes up with the perfect blend and does everything right."
—*The Oakland Press*

"Wickedly sassy humor…
Britton is an up-and-coming romance writer."
—*Library Journal*

Dear Reader,

Well, here it is—my second book for Harlequin's American Romance. Woo-hoo! But I'm even more excited to report that I've been signed to write three more books for Harlequin, books about—what else?—cowboys.

In the meantime, I hope you enjoy *Cowboy Trouble*, the story of a stock contractor, down on his luck, who's suddenly propelled into stardom (much to his dismay), and the feisty PR agent brought in to handle the mess. It was a lot of fun to write. I hope you enjoy it, too. And if you get a chance, pick up the book's prequel, *Cowboy Lessons* (September 2003), another one I loved writing.

Wishing you all the best this fall. May all your books be keepers that bring smiles to your face and love to your heart.

Pamela Britton

COWBOY TROUBLE
Pamela Britton

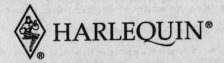
HARLEQUIN®

TORONTO • NEW YORK • LONDON
AMSTERDAM • PARIS • SYDNEY • HAMBURG
STOCKHOLM • ATHENS • TOKYO • MILAN • MADRID
PRAGUE • WARSAW • BUDAPEST • AUCKLAND

ISBN 0-373-75044-7

COWBOY TROUBLE

Copyright © 2004 by Pamela Britton.

www.eHarlequin.com

Printed in U.S.A.

To all my new friends in Cottonwood, California. You've shown me firsthand the marvelous fun of living in a small town. Special thanks to the gang at The Elegant Bean and Barnes & Noble, the two places where I most like to write. And to Dave Tappan of Star 107, Dr. Mendelsohn, M.D., F.A.C.C., and his staff, and to Jeff Davis of Four Star Rodeo Company for helping me with various bits of research. You're all the best!

This story is for Michael—
because he's living proof that cowboys are heroes.

Chapter One

Good thing this was a rental car, Lani Williams thought as she bounced in and out of pothole number 9,121. So far, all of them had been the size of her ex-boyfriend's ego, and that was saying quite a lot. At this rate, her wheels might fly off the vehicle before she got to the Running L Ranch.

"I should've passed on this assignment," she mumbled to herself. "And stayed in New York."

Oh, yeah? And not earned the bonus Mr. Abernathy promised if you complete the job?

"I could have lived without the money."

Like you have been? What about wishing you had a little cushion in the bank? Besides, at least you won't run into Eric the Egomaniac Ex-boyfriend in California.

"Oh, yeah," she answered herself as she rounded a bend. "Forgot."

The small valley she'd just traveled through abruptly opened up. She slammed on the brakes, gravel skittering out from beneath her car's tires. The tiny rental, which could give a MINI Cooper a run for its money, slid a few feet before coming to a stop.

"Dang," she said, straightening behind the wheel. "I wonder where he hides the moonshine."

With the June sun beating down, she had a perfect view of the ranch—or rather, its ruins. A cabin—because she wouldn't dare classify it as a house—stood near a stream that had the good fortune to outsparkle everything around it. The structure used to be…white, she noted with a squint, but was now as bare of paint and dignity as the big brown barn that stood behind it. And yet it was a peaceful scene, with tall oak trees dotting the property, including a giant one to the cabin's left, its branches bobbing in a slight breeze.

"I've got my work cut out," she said, pressing down on the accelerator and shaking her head. Branches flicked shadows across her car as she approached.

A closer look didn't help. Piloting her car across the creek over a pair of board-covered railroad trestles that Lani feared would collapse, she followed a road that ran along a tree-studded stream to her left, then pulled to a stop in front of a yard that was in serious need of a trim. The tall dried grass and overgrown shrubs were a fire hazard. So was the once-white picket fence whose gate hung despairingly off its hinges.

"Dang," she said again as she stared out the passenger window.

Bam.

Lani screamed.

Bam. The fist hit her driver's window a second time. Her foot slipped off the clutch, and the car stalled with a jerk causing her seat belt to lock in place. Flinching, she waited for the air bag to inflate.

It didn't.

"Thank goodness," she muttered, blinking at the dash.

Her car door opened.

"I *beg* your pardon." She turned to the person who'd opened it, only to gulp as she got her first shot of Chase Cavenaugh. She'd seen him on TV, but that in no way prepared her for an up close and personal view of the man.

"Who the heck are you?" he growled. "Never mind." His eyes were the exact color of the blue ribbons she used to win at the California State Fair. "I don't care who you are. Get off my land."

"I—" Her gaze darted from the top of his black cowboy hat, brown hair peeking out beneath it, to his snug-fitting tan chaps and sterling silver belt buckle with a bull on it and some kind of writing. She couldn't help it. Her eyes just went off on their own little thrill-seeking tangent, straying to a certain area that those chaps left exposed—

"Now," he added.

She pulled her gaze back up. To be honest, she'd wanted to meet country music's newest star, even if he didn't exactly want to *be* that star.

"I can't leave," she finally said. "I'm supposed to be here."

"You're a reporter, aren't you?"

"No," she said, gulping again as he leaned down into her boxy little rental and she caught a whiff of him. It was a scent that couldn't be bought in a store, a musky, earthy smell that sent her hormones into overdrive.

"How'd you get in here? The gate's locked."

"Actually," she said, "it wasn't. In fact, I'm surprised one of the news vans didn't figure that out before I did."

"Get off my land," he repeated, his square jaw hard. "I'm not giving any interviews, especially to reporters who trespass."

"I'm not a reporter," she said again. "I work for Abernathy and Cornblum."

"Who?"

"A PR firm."

"A *PR* firm?"

Lani decided it was time to take control of the situation. Well, all right, perhaps that was slightly optimistic. Chase Cavenaugh was one handsome man. And he knocked her for a loop.

In New York, cowboys were a rarity. Oh, she'd seen the odd one at the airport, but she'd never seen the genuine article before. Not this close up, she hadn't. What was more, this cowboy looked like he should grace the cover of a Western magazine—his face was tanned beneath his cowboy hat, his chest was broad and he was highly attractive and utterly masculine. Country music fans—those of the female persuasion—would eat him up.

That was exactly why she'd come here, she reminded herself. She was supposed to divert the press or, if Mr. Chaps here decided, to help him *with* the press, should he decide to accept the fame and fortune that had come his way thanks to a song he'd recorded. One that a nefarious recording studio had recently sold out from under him. Hell, not just one song, but the whole damn album.

She leaned forward to undo her belt. Unfortunately, the thing had locked her into place. She couldn't even reach around to undo the thing.

"Look," she said, feeling more and more trapped by the minute. She tried to get her right arm around, saying through gritted teeth, "I was hired by your friend, Scott Beringer." Each word was punctuated by a jerk on the belt. "I'm a publicist."

"What?"

Forget the belt, she thought, looking back up. "Scott Beringer. Actually, I think it was his wife who came up with the idea. She said you were too stubborn to hire someone yourself, so she did it for you." She looked over at the Robinson Crusoe cabin. "And it's a very generous offer, I might add, because my services don't come cheap."

"Amanda Beringer sent you."

"She did," Lani said, trying to unfasten the belt again by shrinking as far back as she could, only to have the seat belt click her into an even tighter position. Finally, she found the release. She pressed the red button impatiently, once, twice, a third time, until the thing finally popped free. At last. She relaxed, regaining a bit of her dignity. When she looked at him again, he was still staring down at her.

"She said you needed someone to handle the press, and I'm it."

Mr. Chaps blinked at her a few times, then withdrew his head from inside her car and straightened, though he was no less intimidating standing, especially while she sat. He placed his arm across the top of the door frame, his body relaxing as he slowly leaned forward again. The denim shirt he wore strained against his shoulders as he studied her.

Did he like what he saw?

"Go back home, Miss—"

Obviously not. "Williams," she said. "Lani Williams."

"Like I said, Miss Williams. Go home. I don't need help from a publicist."

She shook her head in frustration. "But, you see, I can't go home." If she did, she'd lose out on all the bonus money—but she didn't tell him that. "Mr. and Mrs. Beringer told me to tell you they hired you, so you can't fire me."

"No, but I can kick you out."

Well, now, he wouldn't be the first. "That's true," she said, lifting her index finger for good measure. "But from what I've seen parked outside your front gate—reporters, news vans, curiosity seekers—you're in deep doo-doo. Mr. Beringer tells me you've had people at the house, helicopters flying overhead, telephone calls. You're in the midst of a media frenzy. Frankly, Mr. Cavenaugh, you needed my help two weeks ago."

He stepped back from the door. Lani took the opportunity to escape from the car, her legs a bit wobbly after all her traveling and then the half hour drive from the San Francisco Airport to Los Molina—*not* because Mr. Cowboy here made her weak-kneed. Her black skirt had ridden up, so she tugged it down—casual-like—pulling on the hem of her matching black jacket, too. Above the peaceful gurgle of the nearby stream, the low hum of an approaching helicopter caught her unawares.

Helicopter.

Chase Cavenaugh heard it, too. Lani watched as surprise seemed to make him taller, which made her go back to feeling short.

"It's that damn photographer."

"Is it?" she said, her eyes darting all over his

hard body. "Would you like me to find out who he's with? Ask him to…" Her words fizzled out as he turned away, his feet—booted, she noticed—stomping the hard-packed gravel road. "Hey! Where are you going?"

She thought he'd ignore her, but he didn't. He paused by the worn gate. "To get my shotgun."

"What?" She leaped after him, grabbed him by his very hard arm and turned him around. His feet ground in the packed earth that served as a walkway up to the house. "You can't do that!"

"Why not? This is my land." He motioned to the brown hills and overgrown yard. "It'd give me immense satisfaction to see those no-good reporters crash."

"You don't mean that."

"Actually, I think I do."

She shook her head, the pins that held her bun in place tugging at her scalp.

"Look. Why don't we go into your—" she glanced at the structure he lived in and tried not to wince "—house, where we can discuss this calmly. If that's your friendly photographer approaching, he won't be able to get a picture if you go inside—" another glance at the dwelling, only this time she added a wave "—your house. A picture that might be sold to magazines and tabloids so they can splash a headline across it, like Country Music's Newest Star in Seclusion With Girlfriend, because that's what they'd say, even though you and I have never met before." She looked up. She could see a white dot, which quickly took on the shape of a helicopter. "Or do you mind people thinking you and I are an item?"

He stared at her for a heartbeat longer, then said, "Follow me."

And that was how Lani got a foot in the door. All she had to do now was convince him to let her stick around.

THE DAY HAD TURNED OUT to be one of the worst of his life, Chase fumed as he wrenched open his front door, the helicopter just about on them. The doorknob squeaked in protest. Chase looked skyward long enough to see that a man hung out the side of the chopper, a camera pointed down.

"Son of a—" He pulled Lani inside.

Slamming the door shut, he heard Lani cough and turned to see her wave a hand in front of her face. "Lovely," she said over the sound of the thrumming helicopter blades as she inspected the place, her gaze sliding over the worn furniture of his family room. That was all there was—family room to her right, kitchen to her left, bedroom straight ahead. "I see your decorator went for the earthy look."

She had small arms. The thought popped into his head as he let her go. Really small. "I wasn't expecting visitors."

She didn't answer. Her attention was focused on the ancient and scarred hardwood floor.

Chase followed her eyes and spied a pair of his Jockey underwear, the brilliant white contrasting with the dusty floor. He bent down, scooped them up and tossed them in the general direction of his room. Outside, the helicopter hovered, causing the windows of his house to vibrate.

"Where's my shotgun?" he mumbled, scanning the dark interior of his farmhouse.

"You're not serious about shooting it, are you?" she said, stepping in front of him. She was petite, with striking green eyes. And nice-smelling hair.

"Shoot at it, no. Point my rifle at it, yes," he said in disgust—at himself for thinking her eyes looked striking. Felt like a darn fool.

"No," she said grabbing at his arm. She had a lot of strength for someone so little. "You can't do that. The press would have a field day."

"I don't care what the press says about me. I just want them away from my land."

He tried to move, but the woman had attached herself as stubbornly as a spring tick. "No, Mr. Cavenaugh, you can't."

"Can't? Lady, nobody says I 'can't' do anything."

"Yes, I can see that. But if you point a gun at it, you'll be brandishing a weapon and, having lived in California before, I know that's a felony."

"So?"

"So? Why give them a new headline?"

"Lady, last I heard it was still legal to defend your own property."

"Yes, but not without a reason," she said, moving closer. It wasn't her hair he smelled, it was her perfume; the scent was a distinct improvement over the mustiness of his house. "A helicopter flying overhead is not a reason. Besides, there are other ways to deal with the media." She placed her hand against his chest. "That's why the Beringers sent me here."

Flowers. The word popped into Chase's head. She smelled like flowers, an observation that took him by surprise. He didn't usually notice how a woman smelled. Hadn't since Rita died.

Stepping back from her, he swiped a hand over his jaw, surprised to feel a day's growth of beard. Must have forgotten to shave.

"Be patient," she said. "They'll go away once they realize you're in hiding."

As if on cue, the sound of the rotors changed pitch. Chase walked over to the water-stained window, his shoulders relaxing as he flicked aside a worn brown curtain. Leaving. Good.

"There," she said. "You see? All gone."

He turned back to her, crossing his arms. With her hair bound up on her head and wearing that prissy black skirt and jacket, she looked like a woman who'd been dropped into his family room by accident. Heck, he thought to himself, this whole day's been an accident. No, the whole month. Who'd have believed his damn record could be sold out from under him and there wasn't a damn thing he could do about it? If Rita were still alive, she'd be outraged, too. So would his former rodeo friends, especially Buck. But remembering the friends he'd lost only upset him. The whole damn thing had blown up in his face, and worse, music that he wanted to forget was being blasted in households across the nation.

"Look, I appreciate your wanting to help—"

"I don't *want* to help, Mr. Cavenaugh, I was *hired* to help. By your friends."

"Hired or not, I can handle this myself. The attorneys I've hired have promised me they'll have the song pulled within a week. In the meantime, I can deal with the matter from the business end of a shotgun. Or an Uzi. Or a flamethrower."

"Can you?" she asked in a low voice. "You don't seem to be handling it so far."

"Lady, I'm a six-time world champion rodeo rider. I can handle anything."

"I don't doubt that you used to charm the skirts off the female reporters who followed your career as a cowboy. But, Toto, you're not in Kansas anymore. You have no idea what it's like to be famous—not just a momentary blip on the media's radar, but truly famous. This song from your album, the one that's zooming up the charts, it's caused a national sensation, especially since the story broke that you're trying to get it pulled off the air. America is fascinated by a man who doesn't want to be famous but who suddenly finds that he is. Especially a man who has such a unique voice."

She raised her hand, using it to punctuate her words, "Ex-professional cowboy hits it big with music he recorded years ago." Her hand dropped to her side. "They love it."

Her words made him stiffen. Yeah, he could see how people would think of it that way. But he'd recorded the song along with several others a long time ago—heck, he'd even sold a few copies of the CD to his rodeo pals. That was a different Chase Cavenaugh. Now he didn't want anything to do with fame, or the notoriety that goes with it.

"Look, whether you choose to follow the path of fame and fortune is up to you, Mr. Cavenaugh, but I'm here to help you in the interim. Your refusal to speak to the press has made you even more of a story. People want to know what you're thinking. They want to know how it feels to hit it big. To hear your thoughts on the album being released without your approval. The fact that you haven't spoken makes their desire burn even more."

"Unbelievable," Chase muttered, wiping his face.

"It's a slow news week and this is a terrific human interest story."

"There's nothing interesting about it."

"I heard you had to call the sheriff to get the

news vans away from the house. And that you've had to change your phone number. That you're afraid of going into town."

"*What?* That's a bunch of BS."

"Is it?"

"I was planning on going into town today, as a matter of fact."

"That wouldn't be wise, Mr. Cavenaugh. They'll follow you to Los Molina. But if you drop me at the front gate, *I'll* deal with them. You can go away. Leave town—"

"I can't leave the ranch. Or did it escape your notice that I have a couple hundred head of cattle to feed?"

"Is that what that smell is?"

His eyes narrowed.

She gave him a smile. "I'm joking, Mr. Cavenaugh—Chase," she quickly corrected. "Since you can't leave, I think that's all the more reason for me to stay. You need my help, whether you like it or not."

But as Chase stared down at her smiling face he realized that it wasn't because of the mess he was in that he wanted her gone. No, he admitted with a stab of shock. He didn't want her around because, damn it to hell, he was *attracted* to her.

Chapter Two

He wasn't happy about her being here, Lani thought a half hour later, but at least he hadn't booted her off his land. Possibly because she'd lied to him, claiming that she'd needed to use his phone to schedule a flight out.

She'd bought herself some time. Time she'd use to convince Chase Cavenaugh that he had to have her help, because—darn it—she needed the money. For too long she'd gone without the security of good old-fashioned cash in the bank. She intended to rectify that situation with this job.

"Where should I put this?" she asked as she wheeled her suitcase to a stop in the family room.

The cowboy stood in his kitchen, eating a sandwich laden with enough meat, Lani noticed, to keep American cattlemen rich for the rest of their lives.

He turned, sandwich hovering near his mouth. His tall frame seemed even larger in the tiny kitchen. When he saw her black suitcase, he stiffened.

"Oh, no," he said, lowering his side-of-beef sandwich. "No. I told you, you're not staying."

"I checked on flights, Chase," she improvised—all right—lied. The only call she'd made was to the office to check her voice mail. "And there are none until tomorrow. So, I've decided to help you for the duration of my stay, short as it will be." Which wouldn't be short at all, not if she could help it.

"You can stay in town," he said, turning to face her fully, his sandwich-free hand resting on the worn lemon-colored Formica countertop. At least he'd taken off those chaps. Or perhaps that wasn't a good thing, she thought, noticing the way his jeans stretched around his thighs. They looked as if they were in danger of bursting at the seams because of the size of his, um, muscles. It made her feel distinctly uncomfortable. She looked up at his face, trying not to blush. Gracious, what was it about him that gave her hot flashes? Yes, she could admit it: He made her feel *aware*. His brawniness against her diminutive size. His smell, so different from her own. His manliness. Her femininity.

And that wouldn't do. That wouldn't do *at all*.

"It would be better if I stayed here, Chase. I can handle the media more effectively."

"You can't stay," he said, his gaze sliding up and down her body. Was it her imagination, or did he linger on her breasts? "When I get back from town, I want you gone." He turned and threw his sandwich into the sink, which was already filled with dishes from a previous meal.

"Have you any idea how many families you could have fed with the meat from that sandwich?"

His blue eyes narrowed and, as he stood there, she found herself thinking how silly he looked against the kitchen's yellow backdrop. She doubted Mr. Chaps had chosen the frilly lemon curtains that covered the window over the sink. A woman had obviously decorated here—a long time ago.

"Don't tell me you're one of those save-the-world activists?"

"No, I'm one of those 'starving because I took a red-eye and didn't stop to eat' activists."

He held her gaze for a long moment. This was a man who thought about his words before he said them, Lani realized.

"You're hungry?"

"Famished."

"And you would have eaten the rest of my sandwich?"

"Hunger hath no pride."

"I would have made you one if you'd asked."

Why the heck didn't you offer? she wanted to say. "I'll make one for myself, if you don't mind."

"There's no meat."

She wasn't surprised—he'd likely eaten it all, except for the part he'd thrown down the sink. "And here I thought ranches had freezers full of cow."

"I don't raise *cow,* I raise beef, but not the eating kind."

"What other kind of beef is there?"

"I'm a stock contractor. I supply bulls and bucking horses to rodeos."

"Really?" she asked, lifting her brows. "I'd no idea there was such a thing, but I suppose someone needs to bring all the animals to the competitions. Does that mean you're on the road often? Who watches the ranch then?"

His eyes narrowed. "I'll bring you back something to eat from town."

Hmm. Avoiding the question. "That won't be necessary, Chase, because I'm going with you."

"Oh, no, you're not."

Oh, yes, she was, even though the thought of riding in the same car with him made her feel even *more* uncomfortable.

"I can manage the press if they follow you, and also grab a bite to eat."

"No."

"I'm afraid you have no choice. I'm going whether you want me to or not."

"No."

She stepped toward him. "If you don't take me along, I'll follow in my rental car."

That made his jaw tighten. The next step she took toward him seemed to cause him to jerk upright.

"Look, we can take my car. That way you don't have to worry about the press—"

"I'm not afraid of them."

"Yes, yes, yes, I know. I was just thinking it'd be easier doing it that way—"

"Do what you want," he said pulling his black hat low on his head, like a gunslinger out of an old western. "I'm leaving."

LANI HAD TO RUN to catch him. Blast it all. Why couldn't he see reason? And let her finish a sentence? And earn her bonus.

"Wait, Chase. Please!" As he reached the front door, he turned back to her with an icy look in his eyes.

"I'm sorry to be such a pest," she said, "but the reality is, I'm tired, hungry and obviously out of sorts. So would you please let me come with you? If it makes you feel better, I can get a room at a hotel while we're in town. Please?"

She thought he'd say no again, she really did. But to her delight, he stared down at the ground, shaking his head in resignation.

"Fine," he said.

Thank you, Lord, she silently mouthed.

It was only when he pulled his hand away that Lani realized she'd been holding it, stroking the top of his knuckles with her thumb. The realization made her blush.

"Follow me," he said, opening the front door and storming down a path of dried weeds that had been beaten into submission. •

Once again, she had to work to catch up to him, his back angry-cowboy straight as he stomped toward the gate. Her rental's engine still ticked with heat as they passed it. Taking another path along the picket fence, he led the way to…

"We can't take that," she said when she caught

sight of the white Chevy truck corralled like a swaybacked nag in a one-stall shed.

"Lady, if you're coming with me, this is what we drive."

Her heels dug into the ground like twin diamond-tipped drills. "I'll need a tetanus shot if I go near that."

"So it's a little rusty," he said with a shrug.

"It looks like a demolition derby reject," she said as she stopped outside the garage. A tall oak tree on her left cast shade over the shed and driveway—if you could call it a driveway.

He turned back to her, his arms crossed, something Lani knew from experience was a male human's equivalent of hackles rising. "If you don't like it, take your own car."

"Only if you go with me."

"I'm driving my truck."

I'm. Driving. My. Truck. He was mad at her. Couldn't he see that riding in a truck where there was only one bench seat—one they would have to share—made her think things that were distinctly unprofessional?

Apparently not.

"The press will be looking for you in your truck, not my rental."

"I told you, I'm not afraid of the press."

To which she could say…nothing.

FIVE MINUTES LATER, Lani decided that being in the same room with Chase Cavenaugh was nothing like being in an itty-bitty truck cab with him. The vehicle wasn't as spacious as its modern counterparts. Her desk back in New York was likely bigger. Worse, she kept bouncing toward him as they crashed in and out of potholes on their way down the long, private road that led to the main gate. The search for a seat belt to strap herself in revealed that there wasn't one. It also revealed that she'd forgotten her purse. Darn it. Now she'd have to ask him for money.

She bounced an inch off the seat again, and closer to Chase. So close, she could have held on to him.

Not.

Holding on to a client had landed her in serious trouble before. Not only had Eric nearly gotten her fired, he'd also proven that business relationships should never move into the bedroom.

"How long have you lived here?" she asked to distract herself.

"All my life," he said gruffly, eyes straight ahead.

"And is that why you sing country music? Because you live out in the country?"

She winced. What an idiotic thing to say. If she hadn't been holding on to the edge of the seat for dear life, she would have slapped her forehead.

"I *used* to sing in my rodeo days. But those days are long gone and I want it to stay that way."

And that's all I've got to say about that, she mentally finished for him, because she could tell by the look on his face that the subject was forbidden. Yet Lani couldn't help herself. Maybe it was the way sitting next to him made her feel—aware of herself and her femininity. Maybe it was simple curiosity. "I was really struck by how good you and your band were. Gosh, even the woman who sang backup was amazing. Did you play together long?"

He swung around to face her, and Lani knew instantly that she'd struck a nerve—a raw, bleeding and exposed nerve. "I don't want to talk about it."

Lani cursed herself. Why? Why had she prodded at an obviously sore wound? She shook her head as she looked out the window. She'd done the same with Eric. And Eric had left her because he didn't need her professional advice, or *her*.

"What the—"

Lani jerked forward. Well, actually she thrust her arm toward the dash to avoid falling off the seat as Chase hit the brakes.

"Unbelievable," he said as they came to an abrupt halt at his front gate. His eyes darted from the news vans to the reporters who gathered like carrion feeders waiting for roadkill.

"I told you it was bad."

Obviously, he hadn't known just *how* bad.

Sensing an opportunity to prove her worth to him, she said, "Oh, look, there's *Entertainment Today*." She waved.

"Stop that," he said, grabbing her hand.

She froze. The feel of that man-sized hand clutching her own woman-sized fingers made her gulp. She pulled away and took a deep breath, managing to say, "They'll follow us into town."

"Not if I can help it," he said, pressing his foot down on the accelerator.

"What are you doing?" she asked, pressing her own foot against the floorboard as she worked an imaginary brake.

"Busting through the gate."

"What? You can't do that!"

"Yes, I can."

"But…you'll break it."

"I'll buy a new one."

Lani faced forward, staring at the poor souls who'd been unfortunate enough to stand in front of the aluminum barrier. She waved her hand in the universal sign of, "Get out of the way!"

They must have realized what was up, as they scattered like a flock of ducks startled by a mad hunter.

Boom.

They hit. Lani closed her eyes and covered her face. And then they made a sharp right, which caused Lani to uncover her face and clutch for the seat as she slid toward Chase.

"Oomph," was the undignified sound she made as they collided. "Jeez," she cried, flinging her arms around him and holding on for dear life. "One hundred and fifteen Americans die each day in automobile accidents."

"It was just a gate."

"You might have killed us."

"It was old. Knew it'd give."

"Oh, well, thank you very much. That makes me feel much better."

"You can let go of me now."

Lani stiffened, realizing she'd been all but strangling him. She eased her grip as she very slowly let him go. They were on the main road now—shrubs and trees their only company—Lani's heart was beating so fast she could hardly concentrate on the scenery.

"Look," she said. "They're just going to follow us."

"I know. Hold on."

He pushed his foot down. Lani yelped as the big truck downshifted and lurched forward. "I should also point out that the media would be idiotic not to know where we're going!"

That didn't bother him, apparently, because he kept speeding up. Lani found herself facing forward, statistic after statistic about car wrecks flashing through her head. Sometimes she wished she'd never studied for that game show.

The road into town was windy, the asphalt curving through the hills, which meant more often than not she'd find herself sliding toward Chase, only to immediately slide back in the other direction. She felt like a windshield wiper.

"Brace yourself," he said about five minutes later.

Lani's eyes widened. Brace—

He slammed on the brakes. Her hand shot to the dash to save her from pitching off the seat. Chase stopped with remarkable efficiency, backing up with only a whine of protest from the transmission. In less than ten seconds he'd hidden the truck in a grove of trees.

"This is where Lloyd, our local sheriff, hides out to catch the high school kids who race up and down the road."

Lani blinked as her eyes adjusted to sudden shadow. Sure enough, a few seconds later, a stream of cars flew past them, disappearing around the next bend before Lani could say a word.

Pretty brilliant.

"Stay," he said, opening the door.

Lani resisted the urge to bark like a dog as she asked, "Where are you going?"

"To disguise the truck."

"What? How? Do you have a giant pair of glasses and a nose?"

He stopped to look at her, his expression one of masculine impatience. "Just watch," he said.

Chapter Three

And she did watch him, Chase thought as he pulled up weeds and loose underbrush, piled them in the back of his truck and then returned for more. And damned if the idea of her staring at him didn't make him feel uncomfortable and unusually irritable.

"Can I help?" she asked through her open window.

"No," he snapped, tossing shrubs in the back. The exercise felt good. He flung some more. That felt even better. When he finished, he slammed the tailgate closed. The white truck looked completely different loaded with debris and covered by a bright blue tarp.

"Clever," she said, getting out of the truck to study his handiwork. "You really should take your cowboy hat off, too. It's a dead giveaway."

He had the urge to give her "the look," the one his traveling partners claimed could bring any woman to his side. Damn. He'd almost forgotten about that.

Instead he did as she suggested. "Let's go," he said as he climbed inside. He didn't like how she made him feel. Anxious. On edge. Like he used to feel before climbing onto a bull.

Chase started the truck and took off, accelerating so fast, he almost lost his load. Lani didn't say a word. She just clutched the front of her seat, perched there like a bird on a moving branch. Chase stared straight ahead, trying to ignore that damn feminine scent of hers filling his nostrils. His knuckles tightened. Abstinence. That's what it was. He needed to blow off some steam. She just happened to be the nearest relief valve.

"SON OF A—" Chase skidded to a halt at the Stop sign. They were just about to enter the main drag of Los Molina, one of California's oldest historic towns. "What the hell is wrong with these people?" He looked through his windshield at the media crews congregated outside the coffee shop across the intersection. "Don't they have another news story to pursue?"

The truck idled noisily. It was a hot day, and many of the front doors of the historic two-story buildings that lined Main Street were open to draw in a summer breeze. A white banner hung across the two-lane road advertising this weekend's street fair. The entire street seemed to lay in readiness for a deluge of tourists. Chase usually found comfort in the sight. Today, he found anything but.

"Son of a—"

"Beehive," she finished for him.

Beehive. Yeah, that was it.

"You going to turn around?"

He wanted to, but damned if he'd let the press run him out of his own town. "Change places with me," he ordered.

When he glanced over at her, he could tell she was tempted to say, "Told you so."

He put his hand on the door.

"Don't do that," she said quickly, touching his arm. He froze. She jerked her hand away. "If you get out, you'll draw attention. Just slide across the seat."

Slide across the—

She shifted, squatting in the area between her seat and the dash. "C'mon!"

Chase had a notion that changing places like this might not be the best thing to do, but he put the truck in park and did as she suggested. It brought them tightly together, her upper body against his, and for a moment the interior of the cab felt about as comfortable as a cowboy hat two sizes too small. Her eyes had some blue in them, right in the center, the color bursting outward—

"Move," he ordered, fed up with himself and his ridiculous attraction to her.

She blinked, then looked away, her shoulders brushing his as she took his place behind the wheel.

"You, uh, you might want to duck."

"No," he said curtly. "I draw the line at ducking."

"Suit yourself," she said in the same tone of voice she'd used when she'd told him to take her car. Without another word she put his truck in gear. Chase hunched down despite himself.

The crowd turned toward the truck as Lani started to drive, or rather, their cameras turned toward it. The reporters lowered their cameras when they saw it wasn't Chase.

"Where are we going?" Lani asked.

"The pizza joint on the other side of town."

"Pizza," she said in a dreamy voice. "Lovely."

"It's nothing fancy," he said, keeping an eye out for more press. But the journalists all seemed to have congregated in the same spot, lying in wait near the entrance to town. Lying in wait for *him*.

"Where is it?" she asked.

"Two blocks on the right."

She nodded.

"Damn," he murmured.

"Dinner with me won't be that bad."

He glanced over at her again. No, it wouldn't. But that wasn't what he'd been thinking about.

"How long 'til they leave me alone?" he asked.

"A week, maybe longer. It depends on what else happens that could make news."

Not the answer he'd wanted to hear. He ran a hand down his face. If only his damn attorneys would do their job. But they'd told him the contract he'd signed with the recording studio was legitimate. In exchange for using the facilities, Chase had given the studio ownership of his songs. It was a common practice, and at the time it hadn't bothered him. Fact was, he'd recorded the music with Rita to give to his friends. He'd never expected the recording studio to go belly-up, or sell his songs to a record label. Or for those songs to find their way onto the radio. God help him, he'd never expected that.

"A press conference might get a few of them off your back, but most will likely stay in the hopes of catching you on camera now and then."

Hearing that song again, listening to Rita…

"I can be your mouthpiece, maybe deflect the press and discourage them. In a few days, a week at most, I should think most of those news vans will be gone."

She made it sound easy.

"Turn here," Chase commanded.

She headed down a narrow side street, pulling alongside a two-story clapboard building painted marigold-yellow with brown trim.

"Pizza place is on the corner there," he said, jerking his chin toward the corner they'd rounded before she'd parked his truck. "You coming?"

"Darn right, I'm coming."

LANI STOOD on the sidewalk, her head tipped back, simply inhaling.

Pizza.

There was a God.

She ran to catch up with Chase. She wasn't entirely convinced the more astute members of the press wouldn't see right through his hatless disguise.

So she put her arm around his waist.

"What're you doing?" he asked, pulling away from her as if she'd jabbed him with a steak knife.

"Adding to your disguise."

He stopped. She did, too. They were near the corner, traffic from the main drag passing at a lazy rate. Across the street a real estate office flashed a neon sign that read Loans, Loans, Loans in bright, fluorescent blue. The sign was at odds with the Old West look of the two-story building.

"Don't touch me," he grumbled, setting off again.

"Do I smell?" she joked. Humor was something she always resorted to when she was uncomfortable or at a loss for words. "Do I need a shower?"

"I'm the one who needs a shower," she thought she heard him mutter.

They rounded the edge of the building, an overhang shielding them from the sun. The downtown was charming, Lani observed, with little green and blue flags hanging from street lamps advertising a Western Days Street Fair. There were flower baskets everywhere, and benches every few buildings or so. Each business had its own sign beneath the overhang and they waved in the slight breeze. Cars could park diagonally directly in front. Lani looked down the street. Four blocks away, on the opposite side, various members of the press lounged, some drinking cups of coffee, others simply on the lookout.

"Did you know coffeehouses have been around for centuries?" Lani asked.

"So?"

"The eighteenth century, to be exact."

He pulled open the pizzeria door. Lani stopped, the pungent odor of pepperoni and sausage holding her hostage. Her stomach growled its approval. "Soon," she soothed. "We eat soon."

Chase stared at her.

"I'm hungry," she said without shame.

He shook his head, closing the door behind her.

The pizzeria was as charming as she suspected the rest of the town would be. Most of the wooden tables with benches were empty at this time of day. Lani didn't care. According to her stomach it was dinnertime, not three o'clock in the afternoon.

"What do you want?" Chase asked.

"Large pizza, everything on it, no fish."

"Don't get a large because of me. I'm not eating," he said.

"I didn't think you were."

His brows rose.

She shrugged. "I can eat a whole pizza on my own."

"Really?" He turned to the kid behind the counter.

Lani knew the moment she saw the boy that trouble lay on the horizon, and it wasn't because of the metal hanging from every protrusion on his face. The boy looked at Chase as if he'd just won the lottery.

"Oh, man, Mr. Cavenaugh. Cool. Can you sign an autograph for me?"

"Sean, I've known your family since before you were born. What the heck do you want my autograph for? And what've you done to your face?"

"Yeah, but that was before you became famous," the kid answered, searching for a blank piece of paper.

"I was famous before," Chase said.

The pubescent kid waved a hand dismissively. "No one watches rodeo."

Lani saw Chase stiffen.

"Now you're on the radio," Sean said, slapping a pen on the blank side of a pizza order form.

"No one watches rodeo," Chase grumbled as he signed with a flourish.

Lani stepped forward, looking down with interest at the sprawling penmanship. The local doctor likely had nothing on Chase. It was a pretty signature, despite being masculine and bold. Sprawling yet elegant. That sounded like a wine commercial, she realized.

When Chase stepped back from the counter after paying for the pizza, he bumped into her.

Masculine and bold. Oh, yeah.

Their eyes locked. Everything about Chase Cavenaugh was masculine and bold. He was a man's man, testosterone-filled. His lean, athletic build couldn't be disguised. He oozed a gunslinger's allure that made Lani say, "I'll be right back."

"Where're you going?"

"To, uhh—" *get control of herself, to splash cold water on her face, pull her shirt out of her waistband and flap it back and forth so she could cool herself.*

"The bathroom," she said.

"It's that way," said the kid, pointing to his left.

SPLASHING WATER on her face didn't do a darn bit of good. Lani wondered if she might be better off turning this assignment over to someone else in the New York office.

And lose out on two thousand dollars? That's what she'd clear. And that was just the bonus.

Lani removed her jacket and flung it onto the white Formica counter. It'd dawned on her earlier that she stood out like a city slicker in her Ann Taylor business suit. The bathroom wasn't much larger than a broom closet, the mirror dotted with water stains and what appeared to be makeup. There wasn't much she could do about the shirt except make it look more casual. She pulled it out of her waistband and tied it in a knot, undoing the first three buttons and spreading the collar so that it looked less prissy.

So Chase can see your cleavage.

No, she argued with herself. That wasn't why. It really did make her appear less businesslike. Reaching up, she began to pull the pins from her bun, her scalp tingling as her black hair fell around her shoulders. It curled naturally from having been pinned for hours. She fluffed it.

Preened.

No, she told herself, she did not preen. She was blending in, making herself less conspicuous.

Stepping back, she observed the effect she'd created. Well, she didn't look bad considering she didn't have much to work with. Too bad she hadn't brought her bag. There was makeup in it, makeup she could have used…

Lani!

All right, all right. She wanted to impress Chase. She knew men liked her hair. It was thick and long, something that brought out a primal "me man, you woman" urge. Sure, once they got to know her, men usually decided that the hair wasn't worth the trouble it took, but that was beside the point. She enjoyed making a man's eyes widen.

Maybe that was why her heart pounded as she exited the bathroom. Or maybe it was because she felt light-headed from lack of food. Whatever the reason, she paused to look for Chase in the narrow restaurant. He sat with his back to her, staring out at the street, on the lookout, she realized. She should tell him to let *her* do that, and she would, right after she saw his reaction to the new-and-improved Lani.

"How long until the pizza's ready?" she asked, slipping into the seat opposite him.

He looked up, the expression in his eyes slowly changing as he took in her gaping shirt (which she made yawn open farther by raising her shoulders) and then her face.

"What the hell did you do to your hair?"

Okay, on a scale of one to ten, that reaction was about a three. She tossed her jacket into the empty space next to her, giving him a cool smile.

"I took it down."

But while she was disappointed with his words, she wasn't disappointed with the way his eyes narrowed, or the slow burn that began to flicker in his deep, blue eyes.

"Why?" he asked.

Because I wanted you to see my hair.

"Because I looked a little overdressed for Los Molina."

The door's bell tinkled, and Lani turned toward the sound out of reflex. What happened next was out of reflex, too. She hopped up, grabbed Chase by the arm and said, "Follow me."

"What?" His eyes had sparked when she'd touched him. She saw it happen, a flicker that he had quickly hidden, but Lani didn't have time to analyze what that meant.

She pulled on his arm, leaning down so that they were practically nose-to-nose. "The man who just entered has a press badge clipped to his waist."

And still he resisted. Lani almost screamed in frustration.

But then she heard the sound of the door's bell ring again and again. Lani turned and faced the entrance.

"Uh-oh."

Chapter Four

"Mr. Cavenaugh, is it true you wrote your hit song about your deceased fiancée?"

"Chase, do you plan on going on tour?"

"What are you going to do with the money?"

Chase held up a hand as the light from a TV camera blinded him. A flashbulb went off, just as a microphone was shoved in front of his mouth.

"Mr. Cavenaugh won't be giving an interview today, people," Lani Williams said, her hands held out before her as she stepped in front of him, shoving the microphone away. "We'll release a statement tomorrow."

"Who're you?" a woman asked. She wore a suit similar to the one Lani had just been wearing.

"I'm Mr. Cavenaugh's publicist."

"A *publicist?*" Chase wasn't sure which man

had said it. There were at least thirty people crowded into the front of the shop. A video game spewed science fiction noises behind him, noises that sounded appropriate to the situation he suddenly found himself in.

"My card," he heard Lani say, watching as she scooped up her jacket, reached into a side pocket and pulled out a business card. "I'm with Abernathy and Cornblum, a New York PR firm. Please call my office if you have any questions."

"C'mon, Chase," she said, turning back to him and pulling his arm.

He resisted. He didn't want to run away. He wanted his damn pizza. Lani's pizza.

"Look, can't you just leave me alone?" he asked the crowd.

"Why won't you give an interview?"

"Is it true you have attorneys trying to pull the song from the air?"

"Do you plan on releasing another song?"

"I didn't release the first damn song. Hey!" he cried as Lani spun him toward her.

"Sorry," she said with an innocent look in her eyes. "We'll be giving a statement tomorrow," she repeated to the reporters, her words so loud and strident Chase glanced at her in surprise. Where the heck had that voice come from?

"C'mon," she said again, her look one of steel.

"No."

"You don't want to do this now."

"Why not?"

"Trust me, Chase, you're not prepared."

He squinted as a camera flash blinded him.

Trust me.

He didn't want to trust anybody.

Against his better judgment, Chase followed her, though not toward the front of the restaurant, but the back.

"Mr. Cavenaugh!" a reporter yelled. Chase heard the footsteps as the media horde followed them. Behind the counter Sean straightened, his eyes widening in awe.

"Is there a back door?" Lani asked the kid.

Sean nodded, pointing over his shoulder.

Lani didn't hesitate. She walked around the counter, pulled open a waist-high door and, motioning Chase through, firmly closed it in the face—or the waists—of the more stubborn members of the press.

"Tomorrow," she reiterated. Then she turned toward Sean. "Did you call them?"

The kid looked uneasy.

"Did you?"

His acne-covered face took on an expression of innocence. "They promised me a hundred bucks if you ever showed."

"I'm calling your parents," Chase threatened.

"I'm nineteen now, Mr. Cavenaugh."

Lani stopped Chase's next words with a hand on his arm. "Next time tell me what the offer is and I'll double it."

The kid's eyes lit up. Lani nudged Chase forward, stopping only long enough to scoop up a box near the register.

"Hey," Sean protested. "That's not yours—"

She ignored him, clutching the pizza as if it were prized booty.

"You just stole a pizza," Chase said.

"I just took what you already paid for," she denied.

"We didn't have to run away," Chase said as they all but stumbled out onto the sidewalk. As luck would have it, Lani had parked right beside the side door. The smell of the freshly plucked shrubs camouflaging the truck mixing with the smell of the pizza.

"They wouldn't have let us out the front."

"I wanted to get it over with."

"It's not going to be 'over' that easy," she said, pausing by the passenger-side door.

"What do you mean?"

"Get in," she said, motioning toward Main Street. A crowd of reporters had rounded the bend.

"Son of a—"

"Beach," she finished for him, opening her door.

"THEY'RE NOT GOING TO leave you alone," Lani said as she took a huge bite of pizza, the oregano flavor bursting on her tongue. Mmm. Heaven.

She sat on the edge of the truck's tailgate, the pizza box between her and Chase. They overlooked Los Molina, hidden from helicopters beneath a canopy of oak leaves. They were only a few miles above the town, but it might as well have been a million miles away. The road they'd traveled to get there had been long and winding, the surrounding trees thick and dense. Lani hadn't minded the drive. This was her third slice of pizza along the way.

"What was that?" Chase asked.

Lani's chuckle lodged in her pizza-clogged

throat. She hurriedly swallowed. "Sorry. Still eating."

He'd put his hat back on. He looked better in a cowboy hat, she acknowledged, not that he'd looked bad without one.

"I said they're not going to leave you alone." She held the pizza poised before her mouth. As she looked into his eyes, she caught a glimpse of panic, as well as sadness. It made her consider for the first time what it must be like for him, suddenly thrust into fame.

"They're not going to give up, not until you at least give them an interview."

"I won't."

She used the lid of the pizza carton as a plate, a yellow jacket dive-bombing her gooey slice. "Hey," she said, glad for the distraction as she swatted it away. "That's mine."

When she looked up again, Chase was staring at her in disbelief.

"I like to eat." She looked out over the valley spread before them. From between the trees, it was possible to see the news vans parked in front of the Elegant Bean coffeehouse. At one end of town, a single-story motel buzzed with activity, too; it was obviously a popular place to stay. Each of the diagonal parking spots was filled. A white van caught Lani's attention. She knew from experience it belonged to a TV network, its white satellite linkup pointed toward the skyline. The dish looked like an upside-down mushroom.

Hmm. Mushrooms.

She picked up her pizza and took another bite.

"What do you propose I do?"

Why the blazes did he always ask her questions when her mouth was full. Swallowing, she asked, "Are you willing to listen?"

He thought it over a moment. "I am."

She batted away the stubborn yellow wasp. It was nice here. Peaceful. She had a feeling what she needed to ask would disturb that quiet. Instead she said, "Did you know you can spray a wasp with hairspray and cause its wings to stick together?"

"What?"

She shrugged. "It's true."

Do it, Lani. You have to.

She swallowed. "I need to know if you have any deep, dark secrets the press might uncover."

She didn't look up at him immediately. She hated asking that question of clients. It always made them defensive, sometimes angry. When she gauged enough time had passed for Chase to either erupt or accept that she needed to know, she added, "It's only a matter of time before someone finds out. It's better for me to know now so I can start thinking about damage control."

She waited.

Funny how everything else seemed to wait, too. How the woodpeckers that'd been pounding away at a stubborn tree trunk only moments before, stopped. How the wasp floated away as if sensing a change in climate.

Did he have something to hide? It sure was taking him a long time to answer.

"My past is nobody's business."

Uh-oh.

"What happened?" she asked.

He stiffened, his body rocking back in such a way that she knew he wasn't going to tell her. Sure enough, he pushed himself off the tailgate. "Let's go."

"Well, now, this is a great way to start off our professional relationship."

"What relationship? I didn't hire you."

That made her jump off the gate of the truck, too. Unfortunately, her skirt caught on the edge, the fabric jerked up around her thighs. She quickly shoved it down and looked to see if Chase had noticed. He hadn't. Every muscle on his face was tense; his eyes hard.

"The Beringers were right," she said, flicking her hair over one shoulder. "You can't deal with this on your own. And to be perfectly honest, I don't know why you're looking this gift horse in the mouth. Abernathy and Cornblum is one of the most expensive PR firms in the country. I wish I had friends willing to fork out a fortune just to help out a friend."

He crossed his arms in front of him. "I can pay your bill."

She released a sigh of exasperation. "That's not the point. They're right—you need me. Tell me what it is you're hiding because by tomorrow, or perhaps the day after that, it's going to be the lead story on every tabloid television show. Or maybe you don't mind people dredging up the past?"

He turned away from her, his profile as unforgiving as an Old West bounty hunter. And though she had no idea what it was he didn't want to tell her, the way he stood there—proud and defiant, yet vulnerable—tugged at her.

"Look," she said more softly, "whatever it is, I'm going to find out sooner or later."

He tipped his head back, looking up at the clear blue sky. She followed his gaze. A jet left a trail in the sky, the farthest ends of it melting away.

"A few years back I was involved in a car wreck."

Everything within her stilled. Even her heartbeat seemed to go quiet.

"A friend of mine—she died."

And that was what called to her, she realized. She saw a bit of herself in him. She, too, had lost someone close to her. She felt guilt over that death, guilt she recognized in this man's eyes.

"Tell me what happened."

He didn't want to talk about this and it angered him no end that he didn't seem to have a choice.

Without realizing it, Chase had turned away from Lani, but he forced himself to face her now, steeled against the contempt he expected to see in her eyes.

"I let someone drive when he shouldn't have."

"Was he drunk?"

"Yes."

She closed her eyes for a second. "I'm sorry. Survivor's guilt isn't easy."

He absorbed her words for a moment before he

erupted. "Survivor's guilt? There's no survivor's guilt. Rita begged me to let her drive—or walk—but I told her we were okay."

"Rita?"

"She was a friend. A good friend. And she's the one who died because I let Jake drive."

He looked away for a second.

"You were in the car with them?"

Rita screaming. The car lurching.

He wouldn't remember it again. He would not allow the guilt and pain to gouge a new furrow in his soul.

"Yes," he said at last. There was no reason why Lani shouldn't know at least that much.

"This guy who was driving, was he a friend, too?"

He nodded. "My traveling partner."

"Traveling partner?"

"The guy I drove to rodeos with."

"Did Jake go to jail?"

"Yes."

She shook her head. "Is he out now?"

"He might be. Don't know. Haven't talked to him in years."

He couldn't talk to him. If he talked to him, he would remember. And remembering wasn't good.

"This happened years ago. Do you really think anyone will care?"

"It depends. If certain members of the press find out, they might spin it the wrong way. You weren't driving, which is good, but you were probably drunk, which isn't good. The American public can be puritanical at times. The press might make you appear somehow at fault just to stir things up."

"Let 'em."

She shifted, and Chase realized for the first time that she'd been leaning against the open tailgate. Her dark lashes fanned out from her green eyes, not blinking as she approached him. Her expression made him tense.

"Chase, you don't want people to say things about you that aren't true. Let me help you."

She touched his arm.

He turned away, heading for the driver's side door. "Are you through eating?" he asked.

Sympathy.

She felt sorry for him. What the hell did he need sympathy for? He'd messed up. It was in the past. Over.

Except he'd never really gotten over it. He knew that. Just like he knew he should never have let Jake drive that night. Rita had died. And if he'd just listened to her—the only sober one in the bunch, the one who'd tried to walk home—if he'd convinced Jake to let her drive…

"Let's go."

He climbed inside, looking straight ahead, his hands gripping the worn surface of the steering wheel so tightly that the tips of his fingers turned red.

Rita wouldn't have died.

"Chase, I'm sorry—"

Her words were cut off by the roar of the truck as he turned the ignition and revved the motor.

Chapter Five

The hotel he'd planned to drop her off at was full. So was the next one.

Chase wanted to pound his steering wheel in frustration. Now what?

Every antiques, ceramics and jewelry vendor in the country appeared to be in town for the street fair this weekend. And then there were the reporters.

Damn.

Lani sat there quietly as he tried one more place, a motel he wouldn't let his worst enemy stay in.

What was he thinking? he asked himself as he passed the flashing red No Vacancy sign.

He was thinking he didn't need a meddling female in his life. The only thing worse would be the three old biddies that ran Los Molina's gossip mill. Thank God the Biddy Brigade and self-appointed surrogate mothers were busy helping Amanda with her new baby. Flora, Martha and Edith would have a field day with this.

He rubbed his hand against his chin. She wasn't staying with him.

"You can stay with the Beringers," he said as he turned the truck toward the ranch. The sooner she was gone, the better. "They hired you. They can house you, too."

"I'm staying with you."

He glanced over at her and saw a look he hadn't seen on a woman's face in a long time. Firmness. Resolve. *Understanding.*

He faced ahead, surprised by how her support made him feel. Grateful. Glad. *Like a jerk.*

"That's a bad idea," he said, more to himself than her.

"Why? Do you bite?"

"No—"

"Snore?"

"I don't have room."

"Fleas?"

"I don't have the room," he repeated.

"I'll sleep on the couch," she said, her green eyes the same color as the cornstalks they passed.

"Where you sleep isn't the problem."

"Then what is the problem? Because if nothing else, our trip into town should have shown you that you need my help."

"The problem is that you're—" *Attractive. And you seem to like me, and that makes me uncomfortable.* But he didn't say that. "Better off staying somewhere else." It wasn't much of an answer.

"Yeah, but where?"

"Somewhere," he mumbled.

"Chase," she said. "I'm sorry for upsetting you earlier, but you need to understand that I need to be close by. It's not the regular press I'm worried about. They'll tire of your story soon enough. It's the tabloid press who'll make your life hell."

"Can't you work from a hotel room?"

"What hotel?"

"The Beringer place, then."

"We don't even know if the Beringers are around," Lani said.

"I'll call them," he said.

"Why wait? Let's call them now."

"Fine. Do it," he said.

Lani pulled her cell phone out of her pocket. "What's the number?"

Chase told her, but Lani punched in a different number instead—unbeknownst to Chase. If there was one thing Lani was good at, it was outsmarting men. The trick was not to *let* them know they were being outsmarted.

"The time is—" came the familiar metallic voice.

"It's ringing," she said, smiling at Chase. His truck didn't have air-conditioning, so she'd rolled down the window to let in some of the late afternoon breeze. The air stirred the ends of his short-cropped hair, which stuck out from under the brim of his hat.

"The time is—"

When ten seconds had passed—and she should know; she counted along with every one of them— she said, "I'm getting their answering machine."

What you're going to get is a life sentence in hell for being so dishonest.

"Hi, Mr. and Mrs. Beringer, this is Lani Williams. I was hoping you might let me stay with you since it appears that all the hotels are booked up. Would you please call?" She gave out her cell phone number, and when she hung up, made a great show of clicking the End button.

The smile she gave Chase was one of pure triumph. "Looks as if I'm staying with you for now."

STAYING.

Chase's hands tightened on the steering wheel.

Staying.

Well, he was sleeping in the barn. End of discussion.

When they arrived at his ranch, Chase felt like running down those members of the media who'd taken to lounging in folding chairs outside his broken front gate. Lani, that perverse package of pizza-eating femininity, waved as they drove by.

"Don't do that," he said.

"Why not? I'll be talking to them tomorrow."

He shook his head, looking out his window to the left so he wouldn't be tempted to glance at the pair of long legs to the right. He wasn't in the market for a woman, especially her.

"When did you want to give a press conference?" she asked.

"I'm not."

"You should."

"I'm not," he repeated. The muscles around his jaw started to hurt, he grit his teeth so hard.

Staying with him.

"Look, Miss Williams, you're only staying with me because there's no place else to put you."

Call someone else.

He could do that, he admitted, except he didn't want to impose.

That's what he told himself.

His grip on the wheel tightened to the point that his palms hurt. He didn't want to admit—refused to acknowledge—that he really did need her help. He rubbed a palm back and forth across his pants. No good. This was no good. He'd begun to feel like he used to on his way to a rodeo.

What had he been saying? Oh, yeah. "Tomorrow you need to find someplace else to stay."

"Fine," she said.

Fine, he silently agreed.

They passed beneath the tall oaks, sunlight and shadows flickering over his truck's cab like one of those old picture shows.

Through the break in the trees, he could see his ranch. It looked worn. Tired. Showing its age. Like him. He'd planned to retire there. Fix it up. But he hadn't wanted to after Rita had...

"Damn it."

"What?" Lani said, looking at him in concern.

Impatient with himself, he said, "Nothing."

"What?"

That was the problem. Not only did women distract a man, but they disturb their peace, too.

"Have to feed," he improvised. "With all the hullabaloo, I forgot. Stay here," he said as he pulled up in front of his house. "There's fresh sheets in the closet."

She nodded. He could see that out of the corner of his eye because he sure as heck didn't look at her. Chase hopped out.

Staying with him.

He slammed the door. It wasn't like he'd have to see her often. He'd sleep out in the barn—throw some horse blankets on the hay. Wouldn't be the first time he'd slept like that. Probably wouldn't be the last, either.

Chapter Six

She'd changed the sheets, but it didn't help.

She put a pillow over her head. When that didn't help, either, she got up, opened a window and silently screamed.

What the heck was wrong with her? Why couldn't she sleep? She tried to turn her mind to composing a statement to the press for the next day. But she only got as far as *I'd like to read a brief statement, please...*

He was sleeping outside.

That must be what was bothering her. He slept out in that dusty old barn of his, while she slept in his bed. What she really wanted was for him to come back inside and...talk. As odd as that sounded, she just wanted to talk. Her heart went out to him. She knew what it felt like to have lost someone you loved. First her best friend, Esther, then her parents…

No. She wouldn't think about her loss—or his.

But she couldn't forget the guilt she'd seen on his face, and the way his eyes had seemed so sad as he recounted his story, and how he very obviously felt responsible.

Sleep didn't come easily and the next morning she woke up knowing she looked like something left in his cow pasture. She hadn't wanted to get up, but the sound of pounding startled her into alertness.

Clink. Clink. Clink.

She slipped out of bed—fully clothed in black stretch pants and a white cotton top—because, heaven forbid, there should be a fire and she'd have to dart outside in something that revealed flesh.

Looking out the window she'd opened last night, she saw Chase hooking up a horse trailer.

The sky was a clear blue. It was one of those beautiful warm California days she remembered from her childhood. A breeze blew, toying with the fine hairs on her bare arms. From above, she heard the ruffle of feathers where a sparrow darted from one giant oak to the next. What time was it, anyway? Ten? Eleven? A glance at the clock revealed she'd been close. Ten forty-five. Man, she must have forgotten to set her alarm.

She turned to leave, catching her toe in the fringe of the room's light blue carpet. Snared like a rabbit, she fell hard.

"Darn it," she said, lying still for a moment, her butt stinging. She'd narrowly missed hitting her head on a bookcase beneath the window.

A bookcase.

Dealing With Grief.

She sat up slowly, scanning the other titles.

Losing Control.

When Guilt Rules Your Heart.

Moving On.

And the one that made her sit up straighter: *How Not To Hate Yourself.*

She stared, unable to pull herself away. She didn't know why the titles hit her so hard, well, perhaps she did. Some of them looked familiar.

How Not To Hate Yourself.

Did he hate himself? Was that why he preferred his own company? It didn't take Einstein to figure out that he didn't want her around.

When she emerged from the house a short while later, Chase was still pounding away at the trailer. He must not have heard her because he didn't look up, which gave her time to observe his standard cowboy garb—tan hat, light blue cotton shirt…

Skintight jeans.

Really skintight jeans.

Lani.

Well, she could look, couldn't she? It didn't mean she would touch. He had his cute little rear pointed right toward her, his pockets ready to pop their gold-thread seams as he bent over a trailer hitch that appeared to be stuck. She told herself she needed to keep things professional. She'd even dressed herself in the armor of another black suit, this one with an off-white silk shirt beneath. Yet she couldn't help but wonder if he'd mind her standing there. So she could stare. At him. For days.

She cleared her throat. "Mr. Cavenaugh," she said, her heels teetering on the pebbles of his driveway. She hadn't heard him move his truck.

"Are you going somewhere?" she asked when he didn't look up.

He smacked the hitch with more force than before, as if he envisioned something other than the hitch beneath his hammer. Hmm. But the extra force must have worked. Something popped into place. He tossed the mallet to the side, straightened and turned to face her.

A film of sweat covered his face. Normally, she wouldn't consider sweat particularly attractive, but on Chase it looked great—like the water they squirted on the faces of male models. His arm muscles bulged, from the recent exercise. And he had the cutest hint of a mustache beneath his nose and beard on his chin, a dark shadow that made him look twice as sexy.

She blushed.

"I am."

He was? He was what? "You are?"

"Going someplace."

"Oh." Yes. Jeez, he must think her brain-dead.

"Where, if you don't mind my asking?"

"I do," he said.

"You do?" She was obviously rattled.

"I don't want anyone to know."

She straightened, the professional publicist in her coming to her rescue. *Finally.*

Crossing her arms in front of her, she pasted a look of stern disapproval on her face.

"Mr. Cavenaugh, I insist you tell me where you're going."

"No."

"Why not?"

"Because it's none of your business."

She narrowed her eyes. "If you don't tell me, I'm going to follow you."

"No, you're not."

"Try me."

They stared at each other in a silent battle of wills, one that Lani staunchly refused to back down from.

Finally, he shook his head, the look on his face one of resignation. "I'm taking Hellraiser to visit some third-graders."

Her brows drew together. "You're taking a what to visit who?"

"Hellraiser."

Her brows lifted.

"He's a bull."

"You're taking a bull to visit *third-graders?*" And when he nodded, she added, "Are you crazy?"

"No," he said. Was it her imagination, or did she hear a bit of a laugh in that voice? No. She must be imagining it. He was such a grump it was hard to imagine him with a sense of humor.

"Then why are you taking a bull to visit children?"

"Hellraiser might've been voted bull of the year three times, but he's as tame as a horse."

"So you take him to school?"

"Once a year. Yeah. As part of Western Days. The kids love him."

She just looked at Chase. But as she did, her press agent's mind started to work away. What a perfect place for a press conference. A school. A field of children. Clean, smiling faces.

Please leave this poor cowboy alone so he can continue doing his good works.

"What time do you have to be there?"

"Three."

"Perfect."

He tipped his hat back. "Perfect for what?"

"That gives us four hours to gather the press."

"Whoa, whoa, whoa. I don't want a press conference."

"Why not?"

He took his hat off and wiped his brow. "This is private. Something I like to do. Alone." He narrowed his eyes.

"You'll be followed."

"No I won't."

"How do you know that?"

"Because they'll be distracted."

"By what?"

"*You.*"

THE REPORTERS TOOK the bait, as Chase had known they would. At the same time Lani held a press conference at the Frontier Inn, he rolled away from his ranch, not a single news van, reporter or helicopter in pursuit.

Maybe she'd be good for something after all. She seemed to know what she was doing.

And she's pretty.

He clamped down on that unwanted thought. No entanglements, even the one-night-stand kind.

He made good time. Chase went around to the back of the single-story building. One of their local politicians had moved heaven and earth to get the funding to erect a state-of-the-art grade school. The result was ten acres nestled at the base of the foothills—half of it under concrete, the other half grass. He pulled onto that field now, where the other Western Days Safety Fair contributors were already gathered: a few police officers with their police dogs and cars, firefighters with their red truck parked near the car they'd take great pleasure in cutting open during a mock rescue later in the day. The county hospital's rescue helicopter sat like a monument on Chase's right, the pilot and another crew member standing nearby. Same crowd as always.

"Praise the Lord, he has risen."

Chase groaned when he heard the sassy voice as he was getting out of his truck.

"Look out, girls, it's the second coming," said another voice.

Chase turned. Sure enough, the Biddy Brigade was coming toward him. Edith was first in line, with her long gray braid hanging down her back. Close behind followed Flora, with her recently dyed hair glowing an improbable shade of crimson in the sun, and Martha, the most matronly of the three, her Mrs. Claus body moving toward him at an impressive speed.

Ah, hell.

"Ladies," he said. "If you don't watch out, the Good Lord might strike you down for such blasphemy."

"If He hasn't done it yet," Flora said, "He ain't likely to do it now."

"Who'd have thought a kid I used to spank for stealing my cookies would become a national celebrity," Edith said.

"Is it true you're dating Britney Spears?" Martha asked.

"Dating Brit—" He groaned aloud. "I'm not dating anyone."

"That's not what Edith says," responded Flora. "She saw you coming out of Harry's Pizza with a woman on your arm."

"That's not a woman," he swiftly corrected. "That's a thorn in my side."

All three stared at him with raised eyebrows. Chase felt himself blush. *Blush.* As if he were ten again and they'd caught him in that outhouse with the girlie magazines.

Walt, the county sheriff, walked up at that moment, his walrus face wreathed in a cheek-bulging smile.

"It's Garth Brooks in the flesh," he teased, removing the giant mirrored sunglasses that seemed to be standard issue for sheriffs throughout the United States. Chase ought to know. He'd had run-ins with just about every one of them.

"Or should I call you Travis Tritt?" he asked, his big paunch shaking beneath his tan shirt as he giggled in a way that seemed completely at odds with such a big man. A little boy's giggle.

"Shut up, Walt."

"He's not happy being a celebrity," Martha said. "Speaking of which, how did it come about? Amanda told me you had no idea someone had bought your songs."

"I didn't," Chase grumbled.

"Is it true the recording studio owns the rights?" Flora asked.

"It's true."

"How can that be?" Edith asked next.

"It was part of the deal to use the studio for free." That got Chase mad all over again. Damn it, all he'd wanted to do was record a few songs for his buddies and look where it'd gotten him.

"That stinks," Flora said.

"Boy, doesn't it," Walt agreed, his big belly shaking again as he laughed, his hands hooked in his black belt. His gold sheriff's star caught the sun as he rocked back on his heels. "You're causing quite a stir. Can't turn on one of those entertainment shows or a radio without some mention of you or your song."

"You going on tour?" Flora asked.

Chase released an exasperated breath. "Hell, guys, I just want it all to go away."

"That's what I've been telling people," Walt said. "Here, let me help you with that."

Together Walt and Chase unhooked the portable pipe panels from the side of the trailer. The three biddies melted away, likely to repeat Chase's words to everyone within a twenty-mile radius.

Hell.

It took the two of them only a few minutes to latch the pieces together to form a pen off the back of the stock trailer. Hellraiser unloaded like a rope horse at a rodeo, stopping to sniff the air once his hooves sank into the deep grass.

"Nothin' but soccer balls and little kids today, buddy," Chase murmured to him. "Same as last year."

As if understanding the words, the bull lowered his head.

"Seriously, Chase," Walt said, resting his hands on the pipe panels. "What the hell do you plan to do?"

"I've got attorneys working on that."

"You know, a lot of people would kill to be in your shoes."

"You forget, Walt, I was in the limelight once before, and it damn near ruined my life."

But his longtime friend wasn't looking at him. He was looking toward the road, an appreciative leer on his face.

"Well, well, well," he said. "I wonder who that is."

Chase followed the sheriff's gaze.

Ah, hell.

"It's the press agent Scott and Amanda hired for me."

"That was mighty nice of them."

Yeah, it was, and he'd have to call and arrange to pay her firm's bill since it looked like she'd be sticking around.

"Shoot, buddy, forget her handling the press. I'd let her handle *me.*" He giggled again, walking off after clapping Chase on the back with enough force to make him stumble.

Handle him. Not in this lifetime.

"Did you know," Lani said after stopping in the shadow of his stock trailer, "that the reason Levi-Strauss dyed jeans dark blue was because it was the easiest color to use as a dye back then?"

"What are you doing here?"

From Lani's surprised expression, Chase realized he'd been a bit curt. Damn it, he'd let Walt rattle him.

"I'm done with the press conference," she said.

Ah, hell, he thought. He'd hurt her feelings.

"Sorry," he said. "I didn't mean to snap at you."

She tucked her fingers in the back pockets of her jeans, her loose hair swishing over one shoulder as she tilted her head to the left and looked up at him through those blacker-than-black lashes.

"Do you want me to leave?"

He *didn't* want her to leave. And that was the problem. That and the fact that he had felt unexpected jealousy when Walt had been eyeballing her.

"Suit yourself," he said, turning away. He pretended to check the pins used to latch the panels together, even though he knew they were fine.

He was riled.

"Safety fair?" she said. "I thought this was Western Days."

She looked good, he thought as he peered over at her. Damn it. She always looked good.

"How'd you find me?"

She smiled. His gut tightened.

"I asked the owner of the Frontier Inn. Seems everyone in town knew what was going on here today."

Son of a—

Small-town life. Sometimes it chafed.

"What's your part in all this?" she asked.

He looked around him at the various lifesaving

personnel. At the ambulance crew, a half-naked torso lying on the ground nearby. At the teachers who'd slowly begun to join the crowd—mostly women—and who mingled while they waited for their kids to be let loose from the pre-fair assembly.

"The town does this every year," he said by way of evasion. "It's part of the weekend's festivities."

"Ah. I see, because teaching kids to give a bull CPR is a skill that might come in handy someday."

That comment almost got a laugh out of him.

"How'd the press conference go?" he asked, refusing to show her even a smile.

"Fabulous."

"Over early, isn't it?"

"It only takes two minutes to read a statement. I even had time to go back to the ranch to change my clothes."

He nodded. Obviously.

"Actually," she said, crossing her arms as she stabbed at a patch of grass with her toe, "I managed to get quite a bit done today."

He'd heard her on that cell phone of hers while he'd made himself lunch—and just as quickly left when he'd caught her floral scent.

"Well, aren't you going to ask me what I did?"

He shook his head.

She shook her head, too, rolling her eyes. "I called *Entertainment Today,* told them you're not interested in talking to them. Returned the calls of several morning shows, most of which were already aware that I'd taken over as publicist. Word spreads quickly in this business."

About as fast as it spread around this town, Chase thought.

"I told them you weren't much of a story. That you had no interest in fame or fortune. They seemed to buy it, especially since I gave them a copy of the letter your lawyers drafted, the one demanding the recall of your song. My cell phone hasn't rung in the past half hour."

He felt something stir inside that took him a moment to recognize. Hope. It'd been a long time since he'd felt it.

"Are you going to tell me what you do with that bull, or do I have to wait to find out?"

Hell, the news that the press might be backing down put him in such a good mood that he turned toward Hellraiser, crossing his own arms as he said, "Gonna ride him."

Chapter Seven

He was going to ride a bull? "Tell me you're not serious?"

"I am," he said.

He shook his head, his face in profile, that square jaw of his jutting out for a second as he fought back…laughter? Could he be on the verge of laughing?

"Ride him," she repeated, her lips torn between a smile and a grimace of disbelief.

"Well, I'm not going to saddle him, just sit on his back."

"He'll let you do that?"

"And let me steer him around."

"You're kidding."

"I'm not."

His bull let him ride him. Well, now, she supposed stranger things could happen.

"And so your point in riding a cow would be…?"

He looked at her. "He's a bull, not a cow, and I tell the kids the bull stopped bucking the day Rita died."

The breath left her. That's exactly how it felt—as if someone had shoved up on her ribs from behind.

The day Rita died.

"It's not exactly true, but in a lot of ways I suppose it is. More importantly, I want the kids to understand that drinking and driving affects more than just themselves."

"Oh, Chase," she said.

Dealing With Grief.

When Guilt Rules Your Heart.

How Not To Hate Yourself.

She looked away. Frankly, she had to look away because if she didn't, he would see that her silly, ridiculous eyes had begun to redden.

Jeez, the man took her breath away. In more ways than one. A wounded warrior with a poet's soul, if his songs were any indication.

She didn't stand a chance.

"Can I watch?" she asked, wishing she had a pair of sunglasses. The bull lifted his head, looking the consummate arrogant male, his nostrils flaring, his tail flicking through the air with a whoosh.

"Suit yourself," he said, turning away.

She didn't follow him. She stood there, replaying everything she knew about him, weighing the pros and cons of getting involved.

Bad idea.

Good idea, because if a heart as big as his could be unburied, dusted off...

That's what you said about Eric.

But Eric wasn't anything like Chase.

LANI'S FEAR that the SPCA would show up and take Chase away for riding his pet proved to be unfounded. It turned out that his bull-riding act was an annual event. Everyone watched, from the local veterinarian to the county sheriff.

She'd had to admit that, as a demonstration, it was a good one. Chase made a great show of jumping on his bull. Hellraiser seemed to know exactly what was up. He snorted a lot until his owner settled on his back. Once Chase was mounted, his mood turned serious, and he recounted to the crowd how the bull had magically stopped bucking the day Rita Jones had died.

"This here's a three-time bull of the year, kids,"

Chase said. "He's half a ton of meat and he's bucked off the toughest cowboys in the world. Yet this is what happened when a friend of his died. Just think what could happen to your friends and family if you make the mistake of drinking and driving, too."

If the awe and dismay on their faces were any indication, those kids wouldn't be drinking beer until their first retirement check. Lani almost applauded. She caught Chase's eye. The look he gave her was one that seemed to speak to her and her alone, though what it said, she couldn't say.

She was so deep in thought that when her cell phone rang, she just about jumped over the pipe panels in surprise.

"Lani Williams?" a male voice asked when she answered.

"This is she."

"Lani? It's Ted."

Ted Bohart was a broadcaster, one of the few people in the industry she felt comfortable calling a friend.

"What's up, Ted?"

Please don't ask for an interview with Chase. Please, please, please, please. She hated being pulled between business and friendship.

Was Chase also a friend?

She'd like him to be.

"Sorry to bother you, Lani, but I thought you should know, we're about to break a story about your client."

"It's NOT TRUE!" Chase yelled. "Walt over there, he can vouch for me."

"You weren't driving?" Lani asked again.

"I told you I wasn't."

"And you didn't let Jake take the rap for you?"

"Who came up with that cockamamie idea?"

Her relief was so great, Lani felt her shoulders sag. "I have no idea. I thought you might."

"Hell, Lani, I have no idea. People say the damnedest things."

She looked at the gray school buildings in the distance, the summer sun bleaching them white. She had to squint against the glare. "The tabloid press will be all over this."

Chase didn't say anything.

"They'll make you sound like a criminal, one who escaped justice just because of your local rodeo fame and the fact that you live in a small town."

Chase placed his hands on his hips. "But it's not true."

"It doesn't have to be true."

He looked down at her, his blue eyes so bright in the sun, they were the color of bottle glass.

"You were a Cinderella story—now they'll spin it so that you're the ugly stepsister. It'll keep the story going. People will tune in to learn the latest dirt. They always do."

"Why?" he snapped. "I'm nobody to them. To anybody."

"You won the fame-and-fortune lottery, Chase."

"If I wanted fame and fortune, I'd still be riding bulls and broncs."

He turned away from her, his shoulders so stiff, she longed to work them with her hands, try to loosen them up. Except that it would be unprofessional.

She almost did it anyway.

"Damn it."

"Chase, please."

Please what? she asked herself. *Please don't be angry?* He had a right to be angry. Unfortunately, Chase was learning a lesson few people in the world got to learn. Being a celebrity stank.

"Let's go back to your ranch and talk about this."

"I can't leave," he said, turning back to her. "I have to keep an eye on Hellraiser."

"I'll watch him."

They both turned.

"Shoot, Walt, how long've you been listening?" Chase asked.

"I heard my name. Half the field can hear you yelling."

Lani watched as Chase took off his hat and wiped his brow before replacing it again. "You can't stay here," he said. "What if you get a call?"

"I'm off duty. Besides, you know Hellraiser won't budge an inch for the rest of the day. Go," the man said, waving his hands.

Lani waited to see what Chase would do, waited to see if he'd listen to her or handle this himself. He hadn't exactly seemed thrilled to have her around.

But then he surprised her. Giving her a glance, one edged with panic, he said, "Fine. Let's go."

CHASE DROVE. He didn't give Lani a choice, just opened the door of her rental and motioned her in. She didn't protest.

His knees smacked the bottom of the dash before he jerked his seat back, but Chase hardly noticed. His foot dug into the gas pedal, pebbles from the shoulder flying against the inside of the fenders. The school disappeared from the passenger's side window.

"Where are we going?" she asked when it became obvious he wasn't going back to the ranch.

"I don't know."

He just needed to drive. Fast.

She seemed to understand because she didn't ask him any more questions. The whole way there she was quiet, though he didn't know where "there" was until he arrived. Even then, he didn't immediately recognize the narrow strip of road that dipped and then curved back up, oak trees and scrub on either side. He pulled the car off to the side of the rocky shoulder, a squirrel darting away from them as he shut off the motor. Heat turned the pavement into a shimmering gray. This was where his life had fractured apart.

"Where are we?" she asked.

He didn't answer, just gripped the steering wheel as he stared at the darkened patch of asphalt, still scarred after all these years.

Glass. Metal. Rita's screams.

"Chase, I—" He heard her gasp. "We're here," she said. "This is where it happened."

His grip on the wheel dug furrows into the leather.

She was silent for a long moment, and then she said, "Oh, Chase."

He jerked open the door and he got out. Lani did the same.

"We went to a bar that night. We'd gone to a lot of bars after Buck died." And he had no idea why he was telling her about it. No idea at all. Except that she seemed to understand.

"Buck?" she asked.

"Another traveling partner. Died riding bulls. A friend. A good friend."

Lani waited.

"When it came time to leave, she begged me to let her drive. Jake and I, we both ganged up on her. Told her we were fine. But she kept trying to take those damn keys away. I told her she could walk home if she didn't want to get in the car with us. She tried to do exactly that."

"Amanda?" Lani asked. "Scott Beringer's wife?"

And he remembered it all as if it had happened yesterday.

"I made her get back in the car…."

And if he hadn't, she wouldn't have died.

"Jake and I were laughing on the way home. I thought she was, too." He stuffed his hands in his pockets. "But she wasn't."

She was screaming. Screaming at them to slow down. To pull over. To stop.

He jumped as Lani touched his shoulder. She was staring at him with tears in her eyes.

"It's not your fault."

He dipped his head, shook it, the spot where it happened just barely visible beneath the brim of his hat. There, but not there. A blurry spot on the horizon he could keep out of sight with his head low enough.

"No, but it feels like it. Always has."

"Chase," she said, staring up at him with wide, green eyes. "Don't do this to yourself."

He saw her move, saw her reach up, knew what she was about to do and didn't fight it when she touched his cheek with her soft, feminine hand. She held her hand there, as if waiting for him to react. And for a second, just a second, she thought she might kiss him, but the sound of a car approaching made him step back, his body shielding Lani from the passing vehicle. Wind and debris whipped her hair against his face. The loud music emanating from the car slowly faded away.

"That was close," she said.

Yeah, it'd been close.

"We should go," he said.

"Chase, I—"

"No," he said. "Don't say a word."

"We need to talk about this."

"I don't need anything."

Not even you.

Chapter Eight

What had she done?

What the *heck* had she done?

Lani leaned her head against the steering wheel of her rental car.

You shouldn't have touched him.

She closed her eyes. Chase hadn't spoken a word to her the whole way back to the school. He'd just gotten out of the car, leaving her in the passenger seat without a backward glance, as he headed to his truck and trailer.

Straightening, she started her car.

It was a long drive to the ranch, and by the time she got there Lani had half convinced herself she should pack her bags and leave. Until she spied the woman beside the white truck in the driveway.

Amanda Beringer.

Lani recognized the redhead from pictures

plastered on magazine covers. She'd married her multimillionaire husband last year. But the woman who leaned against the one-ton truck, a faded pair of jeans and a light blue T-shirt covering her curvy frame, was a far cry from the elegant one in the pictures.

"Lani Williams?" the woman said as Lani got out of her car.

"Amanda Beringer?" she asked back.

The women smiled.

"It's nice to meet you face-to-face."

"You, too," Amanda said. Her hair was curly, not straight and sleek like Lani had seen in the pictures. She was smaller than she looked in the magazines, too. Definitely shorter than Lani's own five-foot-nine-inch frame, though she looked better in a pair of jeans and cowboy boots than Lani suspected *she* ever would.

"How's it going with Chase?" she asked, leaning against Lani's car, crossing her arms. "Scott and I were pleased you convinced him to let you stay. That couldn't have been easy."

"I didn't convince him," Lani said, putting her hands in her back pockets, a habit that messed her up when she wore a suit.

"You didn't?"

"I lied to him," Lani admitted. "Told him I couldn't get a flight out until today."

Amanda smiled, unable to suppress a low chuckle. "Good for you."

Lani liked this woman. She made her feel comfortable. As if she could trust her.

"He *still* doesn't want my help."

"Stubborn man. I swear Chase would stand on top of a crumbling mountain, rocks falling beneath his feet, before accepting anyone's help. It's why I took matters out of his hands and hired you."

"That was nice of you. I know my firm's services don't come cheap."

"Yeah, well, my husband can afford to do nice things for people."

For a moment, Lani had forgotten how fabulously wealthy Amanda Beringer was.

"Unfortunately, Chase is going to need my help even more in the coming days," Lani said.

"Why's that?"

Lani filled her in. "It looks as if the tabloid press is going to twist the facts and tell the public Chase was driving."

"But he wasn't!"

"I know," Lani said. "And we'll deny it, too,

but they're still going to say it. And if they find someone who was at the bar that night, someone who remembers Chase badgering Rita to get inside the car—"

"I told Rita to get into the car, too."

The woman met Lani's gaze directly. "Chase isn't the only one feeling guilty over what happened."

Lani resisted the urge to reach out and squeeze the woman's arm. "I'm sorry. It must have been horrible."

"It was."

Lani was quiet for a moment. She liked this Amanda. Heck. She liked Chase, too. He might be gruff on the outside, but she suspected he only acted that way because he was hurting on the inside. Still.

"Darn it," Lani said. "I need to get him to talk to the press. If they meet him, they'll be able to judge the integrity of the man. Maybe it'll help convince him he's innocent. But he refuses to do it. Says it's nobody's business."

Amanda nodded in agreement. "He's supposed to be going to the Cattle Kings Ball with us tomorrow night. Maybe you can get him to speak to them then."

"The cattle king's what?"

Amanda's blue eyes sparkled and she appeared to be fighting a smile. "It's a charity event. About the only event I can get Chase to go to, and *that* only because it's for a good cause. Last year, he served on the livestock committee and I'd hoped he'd meet some nice woman. But that didn't happen."

"Livestock?"

This time Amanda did smile. "It has an Old West theme. The planning committee takes that seriously, complete with pig races, live animal pens and western-style dress. But I wonder if Chase will even go this year what with all the hullabaloo."

"He'll probably go," Lani said, "just because everyone will expect him not to go. He's perverse that way."

Amanda chuckled. "You've come to know him well in such a short time."

"He wants me to stay with you. I was supposed to have left a message for you on your answering machine," Lani confessed.

"A message?" Amanda asked, looking genuinely perplexed.

"I only pretended to call," Lani said. "It's better I stay here, especially with the tabloid press about to converge at the front gate."

"Then it's settled. There's no room at our house

for you," she said with a conspirator's grin. "And we'll have to make him see reason about a press conference."

"How?"

"Let's put our heads together and figure it out."

TWO WOMEN DEEP in conversation always boded ill, Chase thought as he pulled up in front of his house, especially when one of them was Amanda Beringer.

Damn.

"I've invited Lani to the Cattle Kings Ball," were the first words Amanda greeted him with.

Son of a—

"I'm not going," Chase said, even though up until that moment he'd planned on doing exactly that.

"Yes, you are," Amanda called after him.

Chase plunged into his house, ignoring her. He had the same feeling he used to get when he'd jump the side of a chute to avoid a charging bull.

He headed for the kitchen.

The front door opened. "I'm not going!" he called again.

"Why do I have the feeling this decision is sudden?"

Chase turned toward the kitchen door. "Where'd Amanda go?"

"Home."

He heard Amanda's big diesel start up, the sound of the engine filtering through the flimsy walls.

"Good. She can break the news to her husband that I'm not going." He went back to making himself a sandwich.

"You should go to the ball, Chase."

"I don't want to talk about it."

"You're consumed by guilt."

He crossed his arms and faced her. "Is that what you two came up with?"

"That song getting on the air was the best thing that could have happened to you. It rocked your comfortable little world. Disturbed the nest you built to shield yourself from your guilt."

"You don't know what you're talking about."

"Maybe not," she said with a tilt of her head, black hair dipping around her shoulders. "But I know you need to face the press. If you don't they'll be free to spread whatever lies they want. We'll meet them together at the Cattle Kings Ball."

"I'm not going."

"You have to," she said, closing the distance between them. That damn floral scent caught his nose. "Staying here will only make it seem as if you have something to hide. You have no choice."

"The hell I have a choice."

"Yes, you can always go back to the way things were before. Your phone ringing off the hook. Helicopters flying over. Your choice. If you won't play along, I'm gone."

That's what he wanted. Wasn't it? Her gone.

The door to his bedroom slammed.

That's what he wanted, right?

"Son of a—" He stared at the spot where she'd been, his sandwich forgotten.

Things *had* been better. And he didn't want her to leave.

Son of a…

Beach, her voice echoed in his head.

Chapter Nine

The fallout was worse than she'd thought, Lani realized the next morning. Even *she* had underestimated the public's interest in the story. America was *very* interested in Chase Cavenaugh.

Every celebrity TV show in the nation featured him on the previous evening's edition: Country Music's Reclusive New Star Kills Girlfriend. Lani had to admit if she'd heard that headline, she'd tune in, too. A few got it right—that Chase wasn't driving—but they made it sound as if his friend Jake had actually taken the fall for the local hero.

It was a good thing Chase had let her stay, because all hell broke loose.

Lani's cell phone hadn't stopped ringing. She'd spent all morning in her new office: Chase's lumpy couch.

And then the package arrived.

She'd been expecting the information. There hadn't been time before she'd left New York to gather much background on Chase.

What she didn't expect was the way she buzzed with anticipation to open the large brown envelope, glancing outside to make sure Chase was still with his cows before ripping the tab. In a way it felt almost like spying on him as she spilled the envelope's contents onto the coffee table.

Chase's public life lay scattered before her. Newspaper clippings, magazine articles, ads and a video.

Lani examined the clippings first, surprised at the sheer number of them. The sport of rodeo was a lot more popular than she'd thought and, apparently, Chase had been one of its major stars. Five, six, seven years of clippings—and then nothing. He'd simply quit.

The year of the accident.

She slipped the video into the VCR after glancing out the window again. Chase's TV was about the size of a microwave, but it was large enough to see his smiling face after she'd pressed Play.

Smiling.

No, *wreathed* in smiles.

"How does it feel to be a five-time world champion cowboy?" a blond reporter asked.

"It feels great, Anne, just great."

Lani wilted onto the couch as she watched him flirt with the woman.

"Were you nervous getting on Buzzard Breath? You've only covered that bull once before."

"In this sport, Anne, you can't afford to be nervous about anything."

Confidence. Charisma. Sex appeal.

Chase oozed it all. The man had had that special something it took to be a star. Lani sat there transfixed, ignoring her cell phone and the fax, as Chase Cavenaugh's life unfolded in a series of video clips—his first world championship, his second and third, more interviews, a minidocumentary on his rodeo career, a commercial.... She shook her head.

They made him sound like a rodeo legend.

He *was* a rodeo legend.

And as Lani looked around his home, she couldn't help but wonder. Not a shred of evidence remained of his former life. Gone. All of it. Pictures. Trophies. Memorabilia.

Why? It wasn't as if Rita had been part of his rodeo career. Lani knew Rita had usually stayed home when Chase was on the road.

The front door opened and Lani jumped. But Chase didn't even glance at her as he hung his hat on a wooden peg by the door and then made a left into the kitchen. She pressed Stop before he could see what she was doing. She blushed at the thought of him discovering her gawking at video clips of his career.

But he was apparently a man on a mission, banging around in the kitchen, undoubtedly making himself his daily side of beef. When she heard the scraping of a chair against the floor, she stood and crossed to the doorway. Her heart did its usual dance against her chest as she stared at his masculine face. He hadn't lost a shred of his good looks in the years since he quit rodeo. If anything, he was more handsome. He'd lost the trace of good living that had clung to his cheeks. His jaw looked more square, his face more lean. His eyes were the same, though they lacked the sparkle she'd seen on TV.

"I'm not going," he said before taking a bite.

She shook her head. She wanted to make him smile again.

"Up to you," she said, sensing that to push him was the surest way to cause Chase to rebel.

He stopped chewing, his eyes narrowed. He wore a blue denim shirt, the fabric almost the same, exact color as his eyes. That faint trace of a mustache was back again—he must've been one of those men who had to shave every day.

"What are you doing after lunch?"

He set his sandwich down. "Checking fences."

"Terrific. Can I ride with you?"

He stilled, but just for a second. "There's only room for one."

"You only have one horse on this place?" Lani asked. Riding really did sound like a good idea. She hadn't ridden in years. She missed it.

"I don't use a horse to check fences. I use my ATV."

"That four-wheeled thing parked by the garage?"

He nodded.

"Great. I'll sit on the back."

"There's not enough room."

"I thought I saw a rear passenger seat."

His eyes narrowed. "You'll get bored. All I do is drive along the fence."

"It'll get me out of here," she said. "I don't like being in this house any more than you do."

Chase had a red ring mark where his hat had been, which lowered as he frowned. "What makes you think I don't like being in my house?"

"You're never here."

"I am when you're not around."

It was her turn to stiffen, her turn to feel… wounded. The man didn't sugarcoat things, did he?

"Oh," she said.

His look turned to one of impatience, with her or him she didn't know, and she wasn't going to stick around to find out.

"Lani," he called.

She ignored him. Why the heck did she feel so hurt? He was a client. Like Eric had been. And look where *that* had gotten her. Better if she pretended she didn't care that he was avoiding her, and get on with work.

"Lani," he said, coming to the kitchen door, cramming his hat on his head again with a dip of his chin. "I'm sorry. I didn't mean that the way it sounded. This house is so small, there's no room for the two of us. I stay away to give you some space."

Was that just a pat excuse or did he really mean it?

The shadow from his cowboy hat covered his angular face. "You can ride with me if you want," he said, pushing open the front door.

SHE'D FOLLOWED him.

He'd hoped she wouldn't. Darn it. Why'd he open his mouth and invite her along?

Because you felt bad. Because you hadn't liked the hurt in her eyes.

That hurt was the best thing for her. For *him,* too.

Chase started up his ATV while Lani watched. "Get on," he said, revving the motor. The dark green ATV was as wide as a car, but it felt as small as a VW when she climbed up behind him. Her floral scent drifted around them despite the slight breeze that cooled the sunny day and tugged at the brim of his tan hat.

"Seat's hot," she said. Her jean-clad legs pressed into his own, the tips of her breasts grazing his back.

Damn.

Chase revved the engine. He knew for a fact that shaking his head would lead to more questions from her, so he didn't.

"Ready?" he asked.

He didn't wait for her answer.

She clutched his waist as they took off.

He'd wanted her to do that. Shoot. He hadn't

even realized what he was doing—flooring it so she'd grab him—an old trick of his. He slowed down, but it was too late. Lani clung to him as if she wasn't about to let go.

Rita had loved riding on the back of his ATV. *Yeah, think of Rita,* he told himself.

Except this time, it didn't bring the sting of guilt and pain that it usually brought. That surprised him enough that he sped up again, the wind tugging at his shirt and dragging it taut around his arms.

Lani giggled.

He turned his head slightly, wondering if he'd just imagined it.

She giggled again.

He sped faster, telling himself he didn't want to hear her.

She laughed outright now, and he could feel her upper body shake. His hands tightened on the grips. Her chin tipped in close to his face. He leaned forward. So did she. He passed his barn, avoiding the gate that led to the main pasture, riding along the fence line as he did once a year—usually in the fall, when it was cooler—but early this year because…because he'd needed an excuse to get out of the house.

"It's beautiful," she said.

Was it? Chase looked around him for the first time in what must have been years. In the low-lying hills, the grass was so brown it took on the color of dried wheat. Oak trees provided cover for the cattle he could see in the distance. Acres of land. It'd been a dream of his to own the old Gregory place. The rodeo had made that dream a reality.

He expected Lani to ask him a lot of questions, and felt pleasantly surprised when she kept quiet. And so he kept going, following the fence line around the base of a small hill and along the creek in front of his house, down through a dry stream-bed, then back up again. The ATV handled the slow, gradual climb with an ease that would have left a horse sweating, but it made Lani's thighs press into his in a way that had *him* sweating. The steady release and tightening of her muscles was a slow torture, one that brought to mind another kind of steady release and tightening.

Damn.

He paused halfway up the hill for a breather, not from checking fences. With all the hullabaloo in his life, he couldn't believe he felt desire for Lani Williams.

The ATV idled so quietly, he could hear his cattle calling. For a long moment he debated whether to turn back. She had him hot and bothered.

"What's wrong?"

That's when he heard it—the low hum of a helicopter, which in recent days would have triggered the fight or flight instincts in Chase.

"Helicopter," he said.

"They won't see us out here."

He cocked his head so he could see her. Big mistake. With her hair wild from the ride and her cheeks red with exertion, she was irresistible. "Are you sure of that?" he asked abruptly.

"Good point."

He turned the ATV away from the fence.

"Where are you going?"

"There's a grove of trees over by the creek."

"We don't have to hide," she said as he navigated around some rocks. "Really, Chase, I think you should just act as if—"

Her words died as they headed down the hill. Dried grass tugged at their legs. Rocks flew up from beneath the tires. Lani hung on tighter, as the sound of the helicopter grew louder.

Chase throttled the ATV beneath the oak trees along the creek. He plunged the machine into the foot-deep water where the foliage above was most protective and cut the engine. He heard her gasp. That sound, the feel of her body pressed against him—

The helicopter's engine pounded louder and louder, and Chase estimated it was over his house. It hovered there, nearly drowning out the gurgle of the creek as it passed around his ATV's wheels.

Lani breathed in his ear, and Chase had to clutch the handles of his machine. When she shifted, he almost groaned. He wanted to dip his head into the stream, except he had a feeling it wouldn't do a damn bit of good.

A locust let out a high-pitched whine from the branches overhead. He hardly noticed. He was too busy wondering what to do. She still clung to him, her tiny hands on his sides.

"Lani," he groaned. What was it about her that lit him on fire?

This was a sexual awareness the likes of which he hadn't felt in years.

"Ah, hell," he said, slowly pulling away from her grip and getting off the ATV.

As he stood beside her, she looked up. He couldn't look away. Everything stilled, and he knew, he just knew he was going to do something stupid.

He kissed her. She kissed him back, the greedy kind of openmouthed kiss of two people desperate for each other. He bent his head, and their tongues met. She groaned. He pushed into her.

And he was there.

Right *there.*

The kiss turned hotter. Pressed tight against her, he was dying to unzip his jeans and let her touch him, let her caress him, help him to forget…

To his surprise, Lani pulled back.

"Don't," she said, her lips plump from his kiss, wet from the moisture of their mouths.

He stared at her mouth for a moment, wanted to lick at the wetness of her lips. God, the thought of doing that sent a stab of energy through him. He had to hold back another groan.

"We can't do this," she added.

Yes, they could. If they wanted to. He could convince her. He'd always been able to convince women to do what he'd wanted.

But, he reminded himself, that was the old Chase, the rodeo cowboy Chase. The one who'd gotten Rita killed.

"I'm here to do a job, Chase, not—" She shook her head, her black hair falling over her shoulders. "Not kiss you."

He looked down at her, tempted to point out that *he* had been the one who'd kissed *her.* But she was right.

He drew back. She shifted, too. The sound of the helicopter had slowly faded, was barely audible now. Two blue jays fought above their heads.

"Maybe you should go on checking fences without me."

"Maybe I should," he said. But it wasn't relief he felt. It was disappointment.

Chapter Ten

It wasn't a news helicopter, it was Scott Beringer's. Lani could see the logo on the side of the helicopter from their vantage point above Chase's ranch.

"Son of a—"

Her breasts came up against Chase's back as he brought the ATV to an abrupt halt. She groaned, but not because it hurt, but because her nipples were so sensitive, they stung from the contact.

"What the hell is *he* doing here?"

She opened her eyes—hadn't even known she'd closed them—hoping he couldn't feel how tense she'd suddenly become.

"Probably a pep talk."

"I don't want a pep talk."

She almost told him then and there that he had

no choice. She'd taken the decision out of his hands by announcing they would, indeed, hold a press conference at the Cattle Kings Ball. If Chase backed out now, he'd look bad. She'd make sure he understood that before deciding not to attend.

"Chase, I think you should know I—"

He floored it, and Lani almost slid off the back like a cartoon character.

"Chase!" she cried out, but the name was lost in the sound of his ATV's motor revving. Her hands clutched at his midsection; it was either that or fall off. Immediately, she noticed how taut his sides were. Muscles covered his ribs. Jeez, the man was all long, hard male.

The helicopter sat in a field behind Chase's house, its blades still slowly spinning. The owner of that helicopter, Scott Beringer, had made his way to Chase's barn and now stood leaning against it, his arms hanging awkwardly at his sides as if he was confused where to put them. She and Chase zoomed by, and Lani did mean zoom. Chase didn't even slow down. She had a feeling that if Mr. Beringer had been a squirrel, Chase would have aimed right for him.

"Where are you going?" she asked as they skidded to a halt in front of Chase's home.

"I need to clean up," he said. "Tell Scott I'll meet him outside in a couple of minutes," he added, not so much as glancing back at her as he hopped off, swung his gate wide and walked toward his front door. No. Walked was too feminine a word. He strode. The poor gravel never stood a chance.

Lani just sat there, staring after him. The sun beat down on her head, warming her scalp until the heat made her get up and move to a spot beneath one of the moss-covered oaks. A woodpecker pounded the tree above her.

"What's wrong with him?" Scott Beringer asked as he approached.

"He said he needed to clean up." The excuse sounded strange even to her. Well, maybe not. Maybe he was still burning from their scorching kiss, too. Maybe he hadn't wanted his friend to see that. She was almost certain that was at least part of the problem. But she couldn't tell Mr. Beringer that.

She turned toward the man. She'd met the multimillionaire computer genius in New York when he'd interviewed her for the position as Chase's publicist. In her business she met quite a few wealthy men, but she'd never met one *quite* so wealthy as Mr. Beringer. He was one of the richest men in the world—and yet so unassuming.

Kind.

That was the word she'd use to describe him. Kindness emanated from his green eyes. And he still maintained a boyish charm—even when he was on the cover of *Newsweek*.

"He asked that you wait outside," Lani added.

Mr. Beringer nodded, pushing on his temple as if he had glasses on, his arm falling back to his side as he muttered, "Okay."

"Do you want something to drink?"

"Sure," Scott said. Lani noticed little spots of red near the bridge of his nose where glasses had recently rested. That explained the gesture.

"I'll be right back."

Lani didn't particularly want to go in after Chase. Her body still throbbed like a motor with a spun bearing. But she needed to tell him what she'd done about the press conference before Scott Beringer did.

There was still dust floating inside the house from Chase's heavy step. Neither of them had pulled open the drapes she'd closed last evening, and so it took a moment for her eyes to adjust. She headed automatically for the kitchen. He wasn't there. She turned around, only to run smack into his chest.

"There you are," she said as his hands came up to steady her.

"Here I am," he said back, his expression closed. The scent of man-soap, something with cedar in it, drifted between them.

"Chase, I need to tell you something."

"What?" he asked, his eyes narrowing suspiciously.

She swallowed. "Sometimes in my work I need to take matters into my own hands. I scheduled a press conference for you at the Cattle Kings Ball."

"Forget it," he said, trying to move away.

She snatched at his hand, another unprofessional act, but they'd crossed that line beneath the trees.

"If not for you, then do it for me."

"You?" He pulled his hand out of her grasp.

She let it go. "If you don't let me do my job then I'll have to go home. And I'll miss out on the bonus that Abernathy and Cornblum promised."

"What do you need the money for?"

"None of your business."

"Car?"

"No."

"Boyfriend up to his ears in a gambling debt?"

She actually snorted like a pig. She hated when

she did that. "No," she said, hoping he hadn't noticed.

"Tell me why or I'm not budging an inch."

Stubborn cuss. She crossed her arms. Tapped a foot. He kept staring at her, waiting.

"Look," she said, "I just want the money."

"Why?"

"Because I'm greedy and the thought of earning a bonus has me seeing dollar signs."

To her surprise, he smiled, which made her take a step back. Oh. My.

His smile on TV was nothing compared to the live version. It was a smile women usually saw from the pages of a magazine. A smile that was part cocky swagger, part come hither, part genuine friendliness.

"That's it? You're greedy?"

She hated how materialistic that made her sound, but it was true. "I'm tired of not having a cushion in the bank. I was hoping this job would take care of that for me."

"I see."

"Do you?" she asked after clearing her throat. "I can't do this alone, Chase. If you won't do it for yourself—go to the ball, attend the press conference I've set up there—will you please do it for me?"

He uncrossed his arms and straightened, only to cross his arms again. "Why don't *I* give you the money?"

"Absolutely not."

"Why not?"

"Oh, yeah, my bosses would love that." She smiled a false, professional smile. "I didn't do the job I was hired to do, Mr. Abernathy, but Chase Cavenaugh paid me just to go away."

"Then don't tell them. Take the cash."

"That would be unethical."

"Yes, but you'd have the money."

"Do you even *have* the money to give?"

The smile left his eyes. "I do."

So he hadn't spent all the money he'd made riding the rodeo trail. She'd wondered. "I still won't take it."

"Then I guess we're at an impasse."

Lani turned, taking the three steps to his bedroom door. Desperate times called for desperate measures. She entered the room he'd just exited, the sight of his bed doing odd things to her insides. Pushing the reaction aside, she ducked behind the door, pulling out her suitcase.

"What are you doing?"

"If you won't cooperate, there's no reason for

me to be here." The suitcase's lid hit the quilted bedspread with a *smack*. When she turned and headed for the bathroom to grab her toiletries, to her surprise, her eyes burned. Tears of frustration.

And, darn it, she'd forgotten Scott Beringer's soda. Oh well, she'd bring it to him when she told him she was quitting.

Chase stood in the doorway when she emerged a few moments later. She ignored him as she grabbed the dirty clothes she'd stuffed in a corner. Stubborn, stubborn, stubborn man. Why wouldn't he listen to her?

"You're not really leaving, are you? You're just packing your stuff to stay at the Beringers', right?"

Her burning eyes infuriated her all the more. So he wouldn't cooperate. It was no reason to cry.

She turned on him. "I wouldn't stay there even if they did have room."

"Why not? I thought you needed the money."

"No amount of money is worth my reputation, which will be torn apart if you don't start listening to me."

"So I'm not going to the Cattle Kings Ball. That doesn't mean you can't keep working on my behalf."

"Yes, it does," she said, having found her medicine case stuffed beneath the bed. She stared at it for a second before tossing it onto the bed. "If you won't do what I advise, what's the point?"

"You can do other things."

"Yes, but offering you direction is my job," she said facing him. The man gave her a look of incredulity. "I'm supposed to coordinate between you and the press."

The darn stinging was back in her eyes and she refused to let him see it. She went back to the bathroom, jerking her hair dryer plug from the wall before returning. She tossed the device into the bag.

"Lani, don't."

Lani jumped when she felt his hand on her shoulder.

"Don't go."

He turned her around, tipping her chin up, and she was caught. Tears were falling and she couldn't blink them away.

"You're crying."

She shook her head, trying to loose her jaw from his hand, but he held on gently. "I'm frustrated."

"So am I."

"Then *do* something about it."

They held each other's gaze and then slowly, so slowly she hardly noticed it at first, a look of caring came over his face. His gentleness held her. She waited for him to do something more. She waited for him to kiss her.

"Why is this so important to you?"

Who cares? Just kiss me. "Because."

"Why?"

He wasn't going to kiss her. She could tell. Her respect for him rose a notch—a lot of men would've taken advantage of her vulnerability. Not Chase.

"I told you, I need the money." She shook her head. "Every month I scrape by. I'm tired of worrying that I'll lose my job one day and have no way to pay the rent. Just for once, I'd like to have financial security."

"What about your parents? Don't they help you out?"

"They're dead."

She saw his chest expand. He stared down at her from beneath the brim of his hat. "I'm sorry."

"Thank you," she said.

"My parents are gone, too."

She looked away. "It stinks, doesn't it?"

"It does."

She wished he'd move his hand. His thumb was stroking the line of her jaw, the pad soft against her flesh. "I'll give you money," he said softly.

She looked up at him again. "No, Chase. I appreciate the offer, but I don't know you well enough for that."

The words hung in the air. *You could know me.*

He didn't say them. Instead he dropped his hand, stepped back and shook his head. "You're a stubborn cuss, you know that?"

She froze. That's exactly what she thought of him.

He ran a hand over his face. The man looked as if he was about to... But, no, he couldn't be...

"I'm going to regret this."

Lani couldn't help herself; she felt hope.

"I'll go to the damn ball, I'll give the press conference, but that's it, understand? Just one."

Disregarding her unprofessionalism, Lani flung herself into his arms. "Thank you," she gushed, hugging him.

"Don't name your firstborn after me yet," he grumbled. "We still haven't discussed the questions I'm willing to answer, and *not* answer."

She smiled. "Chase, you can talk about whatever you want."

"Good, 'cause that's exactly what I'm going to do."

Chapter Eleven

Three nights later, Chase was on his way to the Cattle Kings Ball, grumpy and out of sorts after spending yet another night away from his bed, and Lani.

But that was a good thing, he reassured himself, leaning back in the Beringers' black, stretch limo. The vehicle was as gaudy as a western parade, what with its gleaming chrome, red velvet interior and fiber-optic lights that traced the line of the roof.

"Don't worry, Chase," Amanda Beringer said. "You'll have a good time."

That was the first of Lani's little surprises. He'd expected her to be in the limo—Lani having been gone all day to set up. But instead, he found the Beringers.

"It's a good location to hold a press conference," Amanda added.

And that was the second surprise. Lani wasn't going to ride with them at all. She was already at the ball.

"You had fun last year," Scott Beringer said.

Chase thought he heard Amanda sigh and glanced over at his longtime friend. She'd put her hair up on her head, though if she were his wife, he wouldn't let her out of the house in that black slip. It was hardly a dress. Chase worried she might have an accident if she leaned over.

"I'm sorry this happened, Chase," Amanda said. "I know you only want to forget the past, but sometimes it has a way of catching up to you."

"Ain't that the truth," Chase said. They were the first words he'd spoken since he'd gotten inside.

"It's hard for me, too," Amanda said. "Hearing those songs, knowing Rita is playing the guitar…."

Chase studied her. Rita had been her friend, too. Ah, hell.

"This hasn't been easy on any of us," Chase admitted.

"I hope Lani has been a help to you."

Chase had to confess, she had been. "I never thanked you," he said gruffly.

"It was no trouble. We knew you needed help."

He watched as Amanda exchanged a look with her husband.

A look of love.

Yeah, well, she deserved love. And the man she'd picked, Mr. Multimillionaire, wasn't half-bad.

"Next time you decide to 'help' me, let me know first. Okay?"

"So you can turn me down? Not on your life, cowboy."

He caught a glimpse of Amanda's eyes. They twinkled with sudden humor. So did her husband's.

"Thanks, you two," he said.

"You're welcome," Amanda answered for them.

Chase kept quiet the rest of the way, tempted to pull his black cowboy hat low over his brow. The windows were heavily tinted, making the headlights of other cars look like muted strobe lights. More than one driver pulled his car up alongside of them to try to stare inside—hoping to spot someone famous.

Famous.

Hardly.

You are famous, buddy. Whether you like it or not, you're famous. Again.

The admission gave him a buzz of adrenaline like he used to get riding bulls. Except this didn't make him feel good. It made his face turn cold, made his heart stop for a moment only to resume hitting his chest like the hooves of a thrashing steer.

Fame. He hadn't wanted it. Ever. But before he'd known what had happened, rodeos were televised, people were asking for his autograph and women were throwing themselves at him. It'd ruined his life.

He squeezed his hands together tight.

It's just a press conference, Chase, you've done a million of them.

He had, but never in front of Lani.

THE CATTLE KINGS BALL was held at an airfield every year—in a blimp hangar, to be exact. The structure was so large it loomed like a volcano sprouted from black earth. There was no blimp inside anymore, but rumor had it the interior was so large it generated its own weather, rain sometimes falling from the ceiling a mile above.

And now look who recited trivia.

A red carpet greeted him when they arrived. News vans were parked to the right. Surprisingly, no one waited for them outside.

They were all inside.

Chase clenched his fists.

The driver held open the door. Chase ignored him, not giving Amanda and Scott a second glance, either, as he thrust himself outside. Now or never, he told himself, the same thing he used to say when he'd nod for the gate.

Cowboy up.

HAIR? CHECK.

Breasts? Check, but Lani repositioned them beneath the slinky fabric of her black sequined gown just to be sure.

Dress? Well, it better be a check, she thought. Amanda Beringer had told her it'd cost eighteen hundred dollars. *Eighteen hundred bucks!* Imagine paying that much for a dress. But she had to admit, it hugged her body to perfection. Well, maybe it was a little too tight, Amanda being somewhat smaller. And the black gown was probably overkill, considering she was supposed to be here on business, not pleasure. But she'd been unable to resist wearing a designer gown for her first time ever, though it surprised her how heavy the famed St. John fabric was.

She tried not to hyperventilate. Heck, she tried not to lose the contents of her stomach, even if it was only four chicken fingers, the only food she'd been able to gobble down as she prepared for Chase's press conference. Plus, she'd reasoned, eating wouldn't help her fit into the gown.

Taking a deep breath, she glanced at her watch before studying her reflection again. Lani slicked back a stray lock of hair that had come loose from the knot at the top of her head. Show time. Chase should be arriving any moment.

Hairspray. Food. Perfume. The smells assaulted Lani's nose as she left the ladies' room, causing her to sneeze. The coifed and bejeweled ladies hardly spared her a glance as she picked her way through the crowd. A country and western band played in one corner of the (literally) jumbo jet-sized building, while people glided by with sloshing drinks in hand. A lot of guests wore western garb with fancy tooled leather and giant silver conchas, which Lani knew couldn't have come from your average western store. Many, like her, had dressed more traditionally, in evening wear. It amused Lani to observe the odd mix of Annie Oakleys and Ivana Trumps.

"…polo down in Florida."

"…five nannies in a year's time. Can you believe that?"

"…I *love* my new Lexus."

Lani roamed through the crowd. The place was packed now. From where she stood, she had an uninterrupted view of the main isle that ran from the front of the skinny end of the hangar to the back. Corrals had been set up on the left with cows, pigs and goats mooing, snorting and baying. On the right were various bars: Mexican, traditional western and a martini bar (this was still the Bay Area). A horse glided through the crowd, a Trigger look-alike with a Roy Rogers in the saddle. Lani wondered what Silicon Valley's best would do if that horse lifted its tail and pooped.

Where the heck was Chase?

The press conference was in a half hour and she wanted to prep him. She *needed* to prep him. This was important—

A cowboy walked toward her.

A *real* cowboy.

Chase.

Her tongue just about rolled out of her mouth and landed on the floor at Chase Cavenaugh's feet. He looked *that* good in his tight black jeans, white shirt, black silk vest and black cowboy hat. Just then the band struck up the low-toned hum of Kid Rock's *"Cowboy."* Had he planned that? The song echoed off the ceiling, the *thump, thump, thump* of the rap song's beat hitting her in the chest.

Yikes.

She looked around to see if any other women were fanning themselves.

"Who is *that?*" she heard one woman say.

"Chase Cavenaugh," another woman answered. "Oh my goodness, it's Chase Cavenaugh."

Oh my goodness, it's Chase Cavenaugh. Lani shot the woman a glare.

He spotted her then and came to a halt himself. She stood taller. Okay, so she thrust her pincushion-sized breasts out. Frankly, she'd spent a precious two hours picking out a dress, hours she could barely spare in the middle of arranging a press conference, and so she'd wanted him to see her looking her finest. Wanted him to see her as a woman. *Female.*

His eyes dropped, beginning a slow sweep from her shoulders and breasts to her hips and legs. She felt that gaze like a hand. It gave her goose bumps. And when he looked back up into her eyes, her heart pounded in rhythm with the song.

"You look—" she searched for the right word as they came face-to-face "—good."

"I'm comfortable wearing this," he said.

She found that endearing. That a man would admit he was nervous—well, not in so many words, but she knew this was as close to an admission of fear as he'd ever give.

Ah, Chase.

"I've set you up at the other end of the building. There are offices back there on the left—"

"You look beautiful."

She preened. She couldn't help the reaction, he made her smile. Widely. She splayed her arms, turned slowly so he could observe the way the glittering gown clung to her every curve. She even batted her eyelashes as she asked, "Do you like it?"

"I…"

She waited for him to pronounce judgment.

"It doesn't do you justice."

Doesn't do you justice.

If she hadn't already been desperately attracted to him, that would have finished her off.

"Thank you," she said, feeling her upswept

hair tug at the back of her head as she looked up at him with another wide smile.

"You're welcome."

She wanted to fan herself. She wanted to tell the women she knew for certain were staring at him, "Mine, mine, mine."

Instead, she said, "The press conference is this way." She led him down the main aisle. "We're meeting in a room that's, fortunately, sound-proof."

He walked beside her, his hand at her back as he helped guide her through the crowd, the feel of that hand on her back somehow comforting. His shoulder brushed her own as they squeezed by a couple. No, that wasn't right. His forearm brushed her shoulder, he was that much taller than she. Tall for a bull rider, Amanda had told her. Lani liked tall.

"Are you nervous?" she asked, yelling to be heard over the noise of the band. They were approaching the dance floor, and Lani was momentarily amused by the sight of the Bay Area's elite doing their best to dance like cowboys and cowgirls. They looked pitiful.

"Cowboy up," she heard Chase say.

He stared straight ahead, stumbling once before he regained his poise. If he hadn't nearly tripped she'd have had no idea that the pressure of facing a gaggle of reporters was something he definitely felt.

Poor guy.

"Look, Chase. The best way to deal with the press is to look them straight in the eye as you form your replies. Don't fidget. Don't put your hands in your pockets. *Think* about what you're going to say, then—"

"Lani, I've done interviews before."

Yes, he had. She'd forgotten. "This will be different. You've got a few local news stations, but the rest are all with entertainment magazines and TV shows, not to mention the tabloids."

He didn't comment. She hadn't expected he would.

"If they ask if you were driving the night Rita died, just tell them the truth. You weren't. If they ask why they should believe that, tell them the police report should speak for itself. I almost asked the Los Molina police chief to make an appearance, but I thought that might be overkill—you know, as if we were protesting too much—"

"Lani."

Lani looked up.

Chase had stopped. "Relax. This'll go just fine."

IT WAS GOING anything but fine.

Damn it, Chase thought, he should have known better than to say those words. The last time he'd done that, he'd been nearly trampled by a bull, had broken two ribs and sat through thirty stitches beneath his jaw. Three days in hospital and four weeks of recovery had taught him not to tempt fate.

Hank Jones was there.

Rita's father.

He glanced at Lani, but she was too busy staring out at the sea of faces, picking the next person to ask a question.

"Is it true you've no intention of returning to the rodeo?"

Chase looked at Hank and saw three years of rage brewing in his eyes.

It took an effort to look away. "It's true," he said, trying to catch Lani's attention.

"Bert," Lani said, pointing to a reporter near the front.

Bert lifted a tiny recorder as he asked, "Is it true you've been offered a record deal?"

The sweat began to build beneath Chase's hat. He could feel it beading around the brim. What the heck was Hank doing here?

"It's true," Chase said. He quickly covered the mike and leaned toward Lani before she had time to point to another reporter.

"End this thing," he said in a rush.

Lani's green eyes widened as she observed the look in his eyes.

"Why?" she asked in a furious whisper.

"Rita's father is here."

It only took her two seconds to assimilate what that might mean.

She stepped forward, smiling at the press in a professional, friendly way. "That's it, folks. I've arranged for you to receive free drinks at any one of the bars. Just show them your press badge."

"Trying to hide from me, are you, Chase?" Mr. Jones bellowed into the chaos that followed Lani's words.

If the man had called out, "Fire," he couldn't have silenced them any faster. You could hear a pin drop in the metal-walled conference room.

"Are you going to tell them the truth, Chase, that you forced Rita to get in the car that killed her?"

Chapter Twelve

Hank Jones hadn't changed a whit in three years, his squat frame still overweight and top-heavy. An upside-down egg, that's what Chase'd used to call him. Nothing had changed. Well, maybe there was less hair on his head.

"Well, are you?" he asked.

Chase stepped to the side of the podium, covering the spongy black mike with his hand. He tried to pitch his voice so that only Hank heard him. "Hank, c'mon. Not here."

"Don't you tell me not here, you useless piece of dog meat."

"Mr. Jones," Lani said, coming to Chase's side. "Please. Can we meet somewhere more private?"

"No," the man said, his eyes as narrow as a charging bull. "He doesn't deserve this to be private."

The old rancher returned his attention to Chase, his booted feet creaking as he straightened himself.

"Hank, I told you over the phone—"

"Were you driving?"

"You know I wasn't."

"I don't know anything," the man said. By now reporters were shifting to get a better view. "You refused my calls, avoided me in town, walked the other direction when you saw me on the street."

"Do you blame me?" Chase asked, forgetting for a moment that they had an audience.

"Chase," Lani said, clutching his arm.

He looked down at her. "This needs to be dealt with, Lani."

"I know, but not here," she whispered, her eyes as panic-stricken as a cornered horse.

A camera clicked. It signaled the start of a trend, the shutters sounding like a field full of crickets as they went off.

One gangly, male reporter came forward, shoving a microphone in Mr. Jones's face. "Sir, what do you know about the events—"

Hank batted the microphone away with enough force to knock it to the ground.

"Hey," the guy said.

"Well?" Hank asked. "Were you driving? Did

your sheriff friend cover it all up for you like one of the TV shows said?"

Flashbulbs went off, the glare preventing Chase from looking Hank in the eyes. "No," he said. "I wasn't driving, Hank. You know that."

"I don't know anything except that the sheriff called to tell me my baby girl was dead."

Chase sucked in a breath.

Broken glass. Screams. Blue and white strobes of light.

He closed his eyes against the memory, struggling not to react as he'd struggled not to react for the past three years.

"You should never have let her get in that car."

Chase met the eyes of several reporters in the room, including them as well as Rita's father. "But I did, Hank, and that's something I'll regret for the rest of my life."

Hank didn't look as if he cared about Chase's grief. Chase understood. He needed someone to blame. Chase was it.

"You should have let her walk home. Instead you badgered her into driving with Jake behind the wheel. That no-good wastrel Jake. The man didn't even get on a bull sober, much less behind the wheel of a car."

Chase closed his eyes again. What Hank Jones said was nothing worse than what Chase had said to himself.

"I know." A hand touched his arm. Lani's. "I know, Hank," he repeated. "Believe me, I know."

The only sound in the room was the low hum of the fluorescent lights.

"Not a day goes by that I don't think of it." Reporters leaned forward, straining to hear his quiet words. "Now if you'll excuse me, folks, that's all I've got to say."

HE ALMOST LEFT HER behind. Lani had to rush to catch up with him, her efforts hampered, in part, by the sea of reporters that rushed them.

"Chase," she called out. But he wasn't listening to her any more than the members of the press. "Chase!" But he was already through the door. So was she a second later, hitting the hangar's asphalt in high heels. Where was he? She swept her gaze to the left. There. Leaving the hangar.

A glance behind revealed that the press had stayed with Rita's father. Good. Well, not good, but she'd deal with it later.

She headed for the exit, the smell of diesel

growing stronger the closer she got to the open hangar door.

"Chase!"

She didn't know where he was going. Likely he didn't know where he was going. As it turned out, it wasn't hard to figure out. The hangar was on the edge of the airstrip, near the interstate. The roar of the traffic drifted back to her. Under a sky dotted with stars, she saw Chase head toward a group of horse trailers used to transport the livestock to the ball. They were all wide open, though the owners were nowhere in sight. Chase disappeared between two of them.

"Chase," she called out again as she moved to follow.

"Go back inside."

He had both hands splayed on the smooth side of a gooseneck trailer, his head bowed as he took in deep breaths.

"I don't think so," she said.

"Go away, Lani. I'm serious."

"No," she said, coming up beside him and placing a hand on his shoulder.

She saw him flex and then clench his hands. He still wouldn't meet her gaze.

"I'm sorry," she said.

Even though it was night and the only illumination near the hangar came from the parking lights that hummed and buzzed nearby, she could still see an edge of pain in his eyes, a hardness to his jaw.

She'd seen the same expression on his face when he'd been in front of Rita's father. She'd have had to be blind not to see the flare of grief, followed by pain and sorrow. The whole room had to have seen it.

She took a deep breath, opened her mouth to tell him she understood, then changed her mind. She did understand, probably more than he knew.

"When I was seventeen, my best friend committed suicide."

He stared at her, and she was amazed how a man could seem so utterly masculine and yet so vulnerable at the same time.

It was her turn to look pained; she let him see it. "When my family moved to New York from California, she was the first girl to befriend me. Actually, she was the *only* girl to befriend me. Eleven-year-old girls from different states are not exactly embraced, let me tell you, but Esther didn't mind. She was Jewish and I think she understood what it was like to be an outsider."

She had his attention now and decided to lay it all on the line.

"I knew something was wrong. I kept telling her to get over it. I was…" she took another deep breath "…too consumed with the junior prom coming up. I hadn't been asked and it was killing me, only she didn't seem to care."

She crossed her arms in front of her. "I think she even tried to tell me what was wrong one night, but I wouldn't listen."

"Lani, I don't need to know—"

"Yes, you do, Chase. You need to know there are other sad stories out there. Stories like mine."

His eyes never left hers as she stared up at him unflinchingly. "She took her own life a few weeks before the prom, and if you think I was popular before that, you should've seen how popular I became after my best friend took her life."

And just saying the words aloud brought it all back. The taunts. The jeers. Kids could be so cruel. "When the phone rang that morning, I didn't think anything of it." Lani inhaled. "It was Esther's father," she said, wondering if she was doing right, sharing this with him. She'd never shared the story with anyone. Not even Eric. It was too personal. Her dirty little secret.

"And when he'd told me what she'd done, my first reaction wasn't grief. I was mad. No, furious with her for doing something so selfish. How dare she, I remember thinking. How dare she do that?"

A hand reached out and touched hers.

"Isn't that just the height of selfishness?"

"You were a kid."

"I was selfish," she said back. "And then came the guilt."

"Lani," he started.

She shushed him with a hand against his soft, wonderfully masculine lips. "Quiet, Chase, let me finish."

He stared at her from beneath the brim of his hat, and Lani's heart ached for him.

"She left me a letter, Chase, me and only me— not her mother, not the dad who'd been abusing her, but me. In it she said she was sorry. Can you believe that? She was about to take her own life and yet all she could say was how much she regretted what her death would do to me, that she hoped she didn't spoil my prom. It made me think, what kind of friend was I that I hadn't even noticed my best friend, my only friend, had been in so much pain?"

Wiping away tears, she noticed absently that the back of her hand was black with mascara. Oh well. "I feel the guilt to this day. I don't think it'll ever go away."

He didn't say anything.

"Sometimes, things happen, really horrible things that we feel is our fault. We convince ourselves that if we'd done something different, we might have been able to change it. But there are no 'do overs' in life, no mulligans—life happens and no amount of beating yourself up over the past will change that."

She stared up at him, the stars above his head blurring. He had such an expression of need on his face she finally had to turn away.

"I know how guilt can eat you up."

She shook her head. "I didn't pay attention, and now it's too late, but I didn't let it ruin my life."

She reached out and clutched his hand. "You have so many gifts, Chase. Don't lock yourself away in your tower because you feel too guilty to leave."

Chapter Thirteen

He watched her walk away, heard her heels click across the blacktop as she navigated between the horse trailers, her black gown glittering beneath the parking lights. He told himself to let her go, that she was just doing what everyone else had attempted in recent years—to get him to move on with life.

Damn, if she only knew how much he'd tried.

Memories intruded. The ambulance. The hospital. The wail of Rita's father when he'd been told the news, and for the first time in a long time, he didn't fight the memories that washed over him. He had to squeeze at the bridge of his nose to stop the burning that filled his eyes, had to inhale deeply as he stood there. He was no longer numb, God help him.

THEY'D ERECTED A ROW of portable rest rooms the likes of which Lani had never seen. Premium potties. Actually, it was a portable office trailer converted into a bathroom. Lani headed directly toward the mirror. She looked a mess. Oh, well. She tried to repair the damage. A wet thumb didn't do it. Nothing could fix what had happened.

It's not your fault Rita's bereaved father crashed the press conference. You couldn't have anticipated that.

No, but she could have handled herself more professionally afterward. Could have stayed behind with the press instead of running after Chase, a man who didn't seem to care that she'd shared something intimate with him. Jeez, the man hadn't even tried to follow her inside. He'd just let her go. Obviously what she'd said had zero effect.

She took a deep breath, grabbed a cloth towel—nothing but the best for the Bay Area's finest—from the stack and dipped it in cold water before pressing it to her eyes. She hoped to reduce some of the swelling beneath. She hated that she cried so easily.

Someone came in behind her. Lani squelched a jolt of embarrassment that some fancily dressed woman would see her like this. She jumped when a masculine face appeared next to her in the mirror.

"Lani," he said.

"Chase, what are you doing in here?" She twisted around. "You can't come in here."

"I was trying to find you."

She sniffed before saying, "Couldn't you have asked someone else to find me?"

"There's no one around. Everyone's at the other end of the building dancing their fool heads off."

Just then a toilet flushed. Lani felt her face flush, too. A stall door opened, and a woman with gray hair came out, her brows raised, staring from Lani's tear-puffed face to Chase's blue eyes.

"Excuse me," she said as she crossed between them.

"I'll meet you outside," Lani said.

Chase stared at her a second longer before nodding his head and leaving.

"Honey," the woman said as she washed her hands. "If I were you, I'd patch things up. A man who looks like that only comes along once in a lifetime."

Lani pressed her lips together, tempted to tell the woman she had it all wrong. She was Chase's publicist.

But she wanted to be so much more.

So much more.

"I CAN'T BELIEVE you did that," she said, stepping off the last stair onto the hangar's asphalt.

"Thank you," he said.

The two words hit her like a stab of static electricity, making her whole body still. Her heart seemed to stop.

"I appreciate that you didn't try to tell me to snap out of it."

She stood there in the designer dress she didn't own, tearstains still blotching the skin beneath her eyes. While Silicon Valley's high society danced in the distance, she felt something stir inside her, something that made her wonder if her feelings for him were reaching levels they shouldn't.

"Thanks," he said again.

The razor stubble was back, more pronounced beneath the shadow of his black hat. His eyes seemed very blue. And they were filled with a lingering sadness.

"Thanks for letting me know you understand."

And what could she do but grab his hand, stand on tiptoe and kiss his cheek. She felt the urge to linger there, to hold her face next to his, to press into him. Instead she simply said, "You're welcome."

He straightened, looking around. She thought he was going to say he wanted to leave. He surprised her instead by asking, "Wanna dance?"

If her heart had been a ballerina, it would have done a pirouette. "I—"

Bad idea.

"—Sure. Yeah, I guess. As long as you understand it's been a long time since I've danced."

"I'll guide you."

She felt a stab of feminine pleasure at the look in his eyes. The sadness hadn't disappeared, far from it. She'd begun to understand that sadness was as much a part of him as it was her. She'd lost her parents. And before that, Esther. And before that, her home state. But it was all just a part of her.

"Lead the way, cowboy."

He did, and Lani found herself at the opposite end of the building a few moments later. A hardwood dance floor was down, a natural wood pole fence erected around it to give it a western flavor. Bales of hay surrounded the stage, making the band look as if it played on top of them. A few people stared as they passed, but they were left alone. So when the band slipped into a slow dance, Lani allowed herself to be pulled into Chase's arms.

Oh, dear.

It was, she realized, one thing to be held by an ordinary man, quite another to be held by Chase. This was how she imagined it was supposed to be between a man and a woman. She felt protected, sheltered, taken care of.

His arms tightened around her, and she snuggled deeper. And although she told herself she should keep her distance—keep it professional— she couldn't.

"You shouldn't feel bad about your friend."

Lani pulled back, looking up into his solemn blue eyes.

"You were young. I don't know many teenagers who would have the maturity to sense their friend was in pain."

She didn't quite believe him, but she loved that he was trying to comfort her.

"Hell, before I found the rodeo, I was the biggest mess there was. Stealing cars. Experimenting with stuff I had no business with. Put my parents into an early grave, my Grandma Rose used to say. I think she was right."

Her heart suddenly felt like it weighed ten pounds, hanging heavy in her chest.

"Anyway. Don't beat yourself up over it."

Oh, Chase.

She rested her head against his chest, wanting to say so much to him. "Did you know Thomas Edison invented the phonograph? And that it was Eldridge Johnson who invented the gramophone that played the flat discs we now call records?" Ultimately, she was a coward.

He didn't respond. She opened an eye and peeked up at him.

"You're full of trivia, aren't you?"

"I studied for a game show once."

He smiled. She could see he did by the way his cheek flexed, the way his lashes closed a bit. Something tipped end over end inside her. She closed her eyes again. His heart beat beneath her ear—*thump-thump, thump-thump, thump-thump.* The rhythm lulled her, made her mind spin away.

And all he did was hold her. Comfort her. Shelter her.

"We're being watched," Chase murmured in her ear.

Lani straightened so fast, she clocked him in the chin.

"Ouch!"

"Sorry," she said, glancing up to make sure he was all right. He worked his jaw, opening and closing his mouth.

"Sorry," she said again.

A gaggle of reporters stood outside the wooden fence. They watched, cameras pointed in the couple's direction, a few strobes of light erupting when they realized Lani was looking their way.

Damn.

Put a brave face on it, Lani. Maybe they didn't see you bumping and grinding with Chase.

Well, she wasn't exactly bumping and grinding, but it was close. And of course they saw her.

Darn it. This was just what she needed—for her boss at Abernathy and Cornblum to see her in all her cozy glory with Chase on the front pages of some celebrity magazine.

"I shouldn't be doing this."

His brows lifted, the front of his hat shifting up, too. "No?"

"I'm your publicist, not your girlfriend."

But you want to be.

"Who cares?" he asked.

"My bosses will."

And I care that I'm starting to feel things for you. I shouldn't be feeling things for you.

"What business is it of theirs who you dance with?"

She glanced over at the reporters, wondering how much to tell him. Finally she decided it was best to be honest. "Look, Chase, I, uh—" Good heavens. "See, I, um, I recently lost an account because I became involved with the owner."

The front of the hat lifted again. "A client?"

She nodded. The slow dance continued, though she realized Chase's arms had gone stiff.

Darn, darn, darn. She didn't want to lose that feeling of safety in his arms.

"His name was Eric and at one point our late-night planning sessions went a little later than normal…"

She hated to admit this, she really did. It sounded so *tawdry.* "We lost the account when he and I broke it off."

When he dumped you.

Yes, well, he didn't need to know that.

"I see."

He didn't look too pleased.

Well, what did you expect from him, Lani? To be happy that you have a habit of kissing your clients?

She glanced at the reporters again. "I should get back to the conference room. I might be able to answer more questions."

Staying in his arms made her want to run away, but not *from* him—with him. Somewhere. Anywhere.

"I'll meet up with you later."

She pulled out of his arms.

He let her go.

He let her go.

And that made her feel such a combination of disappointment and regret that when she turned away, her heart felt like it'd skipped a few beats.

No.

She refused to believe it.

She was *not* falling in love with Chase Cavenaugh. Ridiculous. People did not fall in love in a matter of days.

Did they?

Chapter Fourteen

"She's leaving."

Chase didn't know how Amanda had found him hiding out in the darkest corner of the hangar.

"I saw her heading toward the parking lot a moment ago."

"So?"

The way she rolled her eyes conveyed her impatience. "Don't tell me 'so.' I saw you two dancing earlier."

He shrugged. "So I danced with her."

That's bull, Chase, you wanted to do more than dance with her.

"You're attracted to her," Amanda said.

He shrugged again.

Amanda appeared ready to shake him. "She *likes* you."

He pushed away from the wall, looking around to make sure they were alone before saying, "That's the problem, Amanda, she likes all her clients."

"What are you talking about?"

Chase stared into the eyes of his oldest friend. "She almost got canned for dating the CEO of a company her firm represented."

"What's wrong with that?"

Her reaction surprised him. He had expected Amanda, of all people, to understand his concern. She'd been an employee of her husband's before they were married. Well, sort of.

"It's better this way, Amanda."

"Don't you give me that," she said, stepping closer to him, her green designer gown rustling. "You've been saying that about every woman you meet. They make eyes, sometimes you make eyes back, but in the end they go their way and you go yours."

"And what's wrong with that?"

"That's no way to live, that's what's wrong with that."

Chase's eyes narrowed. "You're one to talk."

"Yeah, but at least I wasn't afraid to let myself go when the time came."

"What are you saying? That I should go after her?"

"That's *exactly* what I'm saying."

It was a ridiculous, stupid thing to want him to do. "Amanda, don't harp on me."

"I will, too, harp on you, Chase. Scott Beringer was the best thing that ever happened to me. I have a feeling Lani Williams might be good for you, too, except that tonight she asked my husband if he'd mind bringing someone else in to work with you."

He crossed his arms.

"She wants to leave for New York in the morning."

LANI WOULD miss the ranch, she thought as she climbed out of her car beneath the midnight sky. It smelled like Chase. Funny how she'd never noticed it before. But the lemony smell of dried grass and moist earth clung to the man. She tipped her head back, inhaling.

She wanted him. Lord, she wanted him so badly her feet ached, if that were possible. That's why she needed to go back to New York. The sooner, the better.

It was a hot, sultry night, the kind that stuck to

your skin like humidity after a shower. Crickets sang their evening song, the sound of their chirping coming in waves; frogs in the creek to her left joined in occasionally. Up above, stars twinkled so clearly, she felt as if she were on another planet. There was no smog to turn the stars brown, just a pristine white twinkling in smudgy constellations.

Chase.

She wouldn't think about him, she told herself as she walked inside his house.

It smelled like Chase.

Think about leaving tomorrow. Think about packing. You need to get your office equipment together. Get your stuff out of his room.

It'd be best to stay at a hotel tonight, leave before he got back from the ball.

One night.

No. You're not going to have one night with him.

She knew that. She couldn't have one night with him, she thought as she packed up her equipment, because if she did, she had a feeling she'd never want to leave—and that scared her to death.

"Lani."

Lani screamed, dropping the pair of jeans she'd been about to toss into her suitcase.

"I didn't mean to startle you," Chase said.

He stood in the bedroom doorway, the bathroom light casting a soft glow on his face, and all she wanted to do was run away.

"What are you doing back so soon?"

"Amanda told me you were leaving."

She started to drag a hand through her hair, remembering too late that it was still pulled back. She clenched her fingers.

Lord, she hadn't even heard the limo drive up. *Too busy mooning over him.*

"Are you?" he asked.

"Chase…" He stepped toward her. "I—"

The look on his face as he approached her, the way his hand began to lift…

"I am leaving," she forced herself to say.

He cupped her face in his hands. "I don't want you to leave."

His thumb found her lip. Her eyes closed, every nerve ending in her body dancing like the end of a live wire.

"That's too bad because I—"

He kissed her. Every protest, every thought, every *everything* scattered. She arched her body into him. She couldn't help it, the reaction was completely involuntary. Her mouth opened in a gasp as he pulled her toward him, his hands on her bare shoulders.

Yes. She had wanted him from the moment she'd seen him standing by the door of her car, sexy, masculine and, yes, she saw it now—wounded.

His tongue found the inside of her mouth. She gave him touch for touch back, kissing him more deeply than any man before, the hot warmth of him making the tips of her breasts heavy. And then he touched her breasts, his fingers caressing the tips, and everything in her stood still. A flash of warmth centered between her legs.

Chase.

Desire rolled through her mind, but something else touched the edges of her heart. He was making love to her, probably making love for the first time in years.

When he stopped kissing, she threw back her head and sucked in some air. Everything spun as he covered the indent near her shoulder with his mouth.

"I want to see you naked."

She wanted to see *him* naked. No. She didn't need to see him naked. She could tell with her hands what he looked like. Her fingers drifted up his arms, feeling the ridges and bulges of a man who worked his body for a living.

"Lani," he said as he kissed the top of her shoulder, his thumb toying with the straps of her borrowed dress. If he kept tugging at the stretchy material, her dress would fall in a pool at her feet. She wore nothing underneath. Just thong underwear and heels…

The dress fell.

She opened her eyes. She wasn't voluptuous— far from it.

"Perfect," he said, his hands caressing the underside of her breasts.

She shivered, not with cold, but with desire. She wanted him to kiss her breasts, to make her forget the wavering uncertainty at the back of her mind.

He wasn't Eric.

Chase stepped behind her and pulled her against him, his breath on her neck. Not the calm, even breaths of a man enjoying a smooth seduction, but those of a man aroused.

His teeth found the side of her neck. She groaned. His left hand reached around to the silky patch of material that covered her.

"Chase," she moaned.

"I want you," she heard him whisper, his tongue finding her ear. Her head tilted, her whole body pulsating.

"I want you, too," she said as she turned in his arms.

Their kiss was the hot, greedy kiss of two people slaking their needs. She touched him, too, first on the outside of his jeans, then sliding under the waistband.

The sweet touch of Lani's hand made Chase cry out. Somehow his pants came undone, somehow he was filling her hand, pressing against the patch of black underwear he suddenly wanted to rip away.

She pulled back, and though it was the dead of night, he could see the gleam of desire in her eyes. She sat on the edge of the bed…

"I don't have a—" Chase began.

She lifted her hips and pulled off her thong, tossing it aside.

"Lani?"

"Don't talk," she said, taking his hand and tugging him down onto the bed with her.

She'd be gone tomorrow.

No strings.

No commitment.

She slid onto him with a burst of heat that made them both groan. He pushed deeper into her. Her arms tightened around him, and he trembled as he pulled back out of her.

"Chase!" she cried, lifting her hips.

He pushed into her again.

"Chase." This time the word was a sigh.

When he withdrew a second time, he knew she was on the edge, that she would lose control any second, that all he had to do was push into her again, hold himself there.

"Oh, Chase," she sighed.

And there it was, the pulsing he'd been waiting for. She moaned with each throb, moved her hips in rhythm with her pleasure.

He told himself to let go, to allow himself the same release as she had.

Except he couldn't.

Chapter Fifteen

Lani rolled over in bed to discover Chase's warm body was gone. She sat up, the morning light turning everything gray. Brushing her hair back from her face, she looked around. The room, with its masculine blue bedspread and drapes were the only indication that a man had ever been there.

Darn, darn, darn. She'd been hoping—

What? To talk to him about last night? To ask him if what had happened was normal. Not the lovemaking part, but that he hadn't climaxed.

Lani wasn't normally an insecure person, but she wondered if she'd done something wrong. If he'd gotten into bed only to realize he didn't really want to be there with her.

It was possible.

The phone rang, not Chase's phone—she'd kept that off the hook to force reporters to call her. Lani wrapped a sheet around her before dashing from the bed to grab her tiny cell phone from the coffee table.

"Lani Williams?"

Where was he? she wondered, pulling back the brown drapes in the family room to look outside. Nothing.

"Lani, it's Phil again, from Network News."

"Hey, Phil."

"Lani, I need your comment on something."

It was a sign of how distressed she was about waking up without Chase in the bed that she didn't panic at the words.

"On what?" she asked.

"Did you know Chase Cavenaugh has given away nearly one hundred percent of his income to various charities?"

Lani's eyebrows rose. "Well, I would just say that demonstrates the integrity of my client, Phil."

"I'll say," the voice on the other end of the phone said. "A half million dollars is a lot of money."

She dropped the phone.

It was the first time in her career she'd ever done that. She scooped up the gray cell, which had bounced off the edge of the wood table. "Excuse me?" she said once she got it back to her ear.

Don't act surprised, Lani.

"Excuse me, Phil," she said again. "I dropped you. Did I hurt you?"

There was silence on the other end until he got the joke. Then the man said, "No, no, no. But I'm still waiting for your response."

What could she say? Holy dog doo-doo ranked high on her list.

"Same as before, Phil. This just goes to show what a truly good person Chase Cavenaugh is. He was devastated by the loss of his girlfriend. He's been trying for years to make it up to her in some way."

"Okay. Well, thanks."

Long after the man had hung up, Lani sat there, the sheet wrapped around her. In shock.

A half million dollars a year.

Where the heck did he get the money?

Did it matter?

Such charitable good works were a PR person's dream.

Chase Cavenaugh, philanthropist.

Chase Cavenaugh, gone, Lani discovered when she finally went looking for him. His truck was missing from the shed.

"HE'S THE LARGEST shareholder in Global Dynamics," Amanda Beringer said less than an hour later.

Lani stared at the petite redhead. "The company you and your husband own?"

"It's a public company—Scott's a shareholder. So is Chase."

They were on her veranda, Lani's phone constantly interrupting now that the news had broken that Chase was a multimillionaire with a song at the top of the country music charts. It was so bad they'd had to go outside to avoid waking the Beringers' infant.

"How—"

"His grandmother," she said, taking a sip of her ice tea. Ice cubes tinkled in the glass like small wind chimes.

"The woman was one of Scott's original shareholders. When the company went public, she made a mint. Scott didn't know of her connection to Chase until after the woman passed on."

Chase wasn't just a millionaire, he was a multimillionaire.

A multimillionaire who was avoiding her. She frowned. The man hadn't even left her a note this morning. She tried not to read too much into that, but it was difficult in light of what had happened.

She was still trying to convince herself that she had what it took to please him.

"That reporter's estimate must be off," Amanda said, leaning back in her white wicker chair with a creak. "By my husband's calculations, Chase makes a lot more than that just on annual dividends. I wonder if he's doing something with that, too?"

Lani looked away, her mind reeling. The Lazy Y looked a lot like Chase's ranch, except it was well kept. What a gem of a property Chase would have if he put some work into it.

Or money.

"I'd ask him myself if he wasn't avoiding me," she mused.

Amanda's brows went up. "Oh, he's not avoiding you," she said. "He's out gathering bulls for a rodeo this weekend. My dad and Scott are helping him."

Lani turned and met her stare. "What?"

Amanda nodded. "I'd be out there helping them, too, except someone's got to stay here with the baby."

Lani stood.

"Lani," Amanda said, sitting forward with another creak. "Chase is...difficult. If what I suspect is true, that you're developing feelings for him, I wouldn't let him run you off. Scott tried to do that to me once. Don't let Chase succeed."

Lani's eyes widened. "Feelings? Oh, no. I just—" Slept with him. "Feel sorry for him."

Amanda didn't look like she believed her. "You're the first woman he's shown any real interest in since Rita. When I told him you were about to go back to New York, you never saw a man fly out of a place so fast. They couldn't bring the limo around fast enough."

TEN MINUTES later Lani pulled her car to a stop near a big aluminum trailer at the back of Chase's property. It had little holes on the outside and bulls cried out in protest from the inside. Next to it were two other trucks and trailers: Chase's, his stock trailer attached to the back, and the Beringers' rig, a shiny affair consisting of a white truck and a matching horse trailer. Lani had to squint to look at it.

"Hello," she called.

Chase didn't look up, just tied his horse to the side of his trailer, the fringe of his tan chaps flopping against his legs. She approached warily, keeping the horse between them.

"I said hello," she repeated.

"What are you doing here?" he asked, and she couldn't tell if he looked up or not because he had on a pair of dark sunglasses beneath his tan hat.

Well so much for good morning. How are you? Sorry I missed you in bed.

"I woke up and you were gone."

She winced. That was the *last* thing she'd meant to say.

"I had stuff to do. Didn't want to wake you up."

Why don't you look at me then? Why don't you smile at me now? Kiss me good morning?

She tried not to feel uncomfortable. Tried to tell herself he was just busy. His lack of interest in her had nothing to do with his lack of pleasure last night.

Had it?

"I just thought—"

We could talk. You could tell me if there's a problem. If I did something wrong last night, because you sure didn't want to talk to me then.

"—we could have breakfast together."

And now she sounded like she was begging. What was wrong with her?

"Already had it," he said as he slipped the bridle off his horse with a clink of the bit against the animal's teeth. He attached a leather halter next, the bridle thrown over his shoulder, his black shirt bunching up at the shoulder beneath the head-stall.

"Oh, well, I—" Don't sound desperate, Lani. So it was a bit uncomfortable between them. "—guess we can have lunch together later."

"Thought you were leaving," he said as he began to ungirth his horse.

"I was."

Were you expecting I'd be gone by the time you returned?

"Something's come up," she said.

Don't let him run you off.

Amanda's words echoed in her head. Well, if he was trying to run her off, he was doing a damn fine job.

"Oh, yeah?" he asked, still not looking at her. Lani was getting tired of staring at the top of his tan hat.

"Why didn't you tell me you were a multimil-lionaire?"

He didn't react, and she was looking for it, too. He just tipped his hat back with his hand before going back to work on the cinch. He hefted the saddle down a second later.

"You didn't need to know," he said as he cocked the thing on the edge of his hip.

"What do you mean I didn't need to know? I'm your press agent. If I'd known I could have deflected some of the bad press by pointing out all the good you've done."

He dropped the saddle at his feet. "What do you mean the 'good I've done'?"

She crossed her arms, telling herself not to feel miserable because he didn't kiss her senselessly.

"I got a call today," she said. "Someone from Network News wanted a comment on the hundreds of thousands of dollars you've donated to charity."

She got a reaction then. His head tipped back, sunlight arching off the lenses of his glasses.

"Son of a—"

She wished he'd take those glasses off, let her look into his eyes, try to glean if he—

Cared.

She shook her head. "I take it you didn't want the fact that you're big on charities known?"

"It's nobody's business. None of what I do is anybody's business," he rested his hands on his hips. "Son of a—"

"When you're a public figure, Chase, every-thing you do is everyone's business."

"I'm *not* a public figure."

"Whether or not you want to be, you are. But that's not the point, Chase. The point is that it's a very heroic thing to do. Most people would keep money like that. Sock it away. That you appear to have given it all away makes you as close to a hero as you can get. At least in the public's eye."

His hands fell to his sides. He shook his head, staring at the ground. When he looked back up at her she was almost tempted to rip those glasses from his head.

What was he thinking?

She couldn't tell.

"How the heck can I go from being a bad guy to being a good guy in such a short time?"

She shrugged. "Welcome to the world of media."

"And this is the industry you work in." He made it sound like an accusation. Like she was somehow tawdry by association.

Don't let him run you off.

"Actually, my job is to deal with the press, which I can do, if you'd be more honest. You should have told me, Chase."

He turned back to his saddle, picked it up and slung it over his back with a creak of leather. The scent of horse sweat filled the air. Lani followed him to the trailer's tack room.

"It's going to keep your name out there longer," she said as he threw his saddle inside.

"Oh, well," he called over his shoulder.

She stared at those shoulders for a moment before saying, "Amanda tells me you're going to a rodeo."

He turned back to her. "I am."

And suddenly, they were mere inches away from each other. She swallowed hard. Wanting to... Oh, gosh, how she wanted to reach up and kiss him on the lips. Tenderly.

"I should go with you."

Want to go with you.

"No."

"They'll follow you."

"Not if you keep them busy."

"They don't care about me, Chase. They care about you. They can call *me*."

"You'd only get in the way."

"So will the press."

"Tell them to leave me alone."

She had to fight the urge to reach up and cup

the side of his face. Ridiculous. She should slap him for being so cold. This was exactly the problem she'd had with men in the past. She was a chump. The moment they started acting aloof, she started acting needy. It had to stop.

"Chase, if I could control the press that easily, I wouldn't have a job."

"I'm going to be gone all weekend."

"Doesn't matter. I don't have anyplace to be."

"What about New York?"

Her temper snapped. She took a step toward him.

Chump no more.

"Look, Chase, I was going back to New York because I found myself beginning to care for you. Except it's too late now. I care." She ran a hand through her hair, stared at the landscape for a moment before lowering her voice. "Whether you like it or not, I care."

Say something, darn it. Say you care for me, too. That last night wasn't just a one-night stand.

But he only stepped past her, going back to his horse. "Suit yourself."

Chapter Sixteen

He was being a bastard. He knew it.

Chase glanced over at Lani as she sat alongside him in the cab of his semi. She looked out the windshield, ignoring him, her profile as perfect as it'd been last night.

Last night.

He shied away from thoughts of that.

"We'll be there in a few minutes."

They were the only words he'd spoken to her since she had climbed inside.

"Great," she said.

She'd done the same—held her tongue—slamming the door of the rig and then ignoring him. For some reason, that irked him.

"Maybe you should have taken your own car."

Her gaze flicked to him with the quickness of a bullwhip. "Maybe I should have."

"There's always somebody in the rodeo willing to loan you his truck."

"Great," she snapped.

"You can leave whenever you want."

"I'm *not* leaving."

He hadn't meant that the way it sounded. Damn it. What was wrong with him?

"Look, Lani, I'm sorry I wasn't there when you woke up this morning."

She looked over at him, then away, shrugging. "No big deal."

Yes, it was, apparently. "I had things to do."

"I know."

But that wasn't the real reason, and he knew it. *Cowboy up.*

"I was uncomfortable with the whole deal," he admitted. "I haven't made love to a woman in—" did he dare admit it? "—years. It scared the hell out of me."

There. He'd said it.

She swiveled in her seat to stare at him, her pretty green eyes unblinking.

"I'm scared, too, Chase."

He looked ahead, trying to focus on his driving and the load of bulls behind him. Concentrate.

They were still beneath the snow level, tall

pines mixing with oaks and maples and low-lying scrub. The soil was brick-red, the gold in the hills the result of iron-rich soil that would coat the hooves and coats of his livestock before the weekend was over.

"Are they still behind us?"

He checked the big side mirrors, the white van still on his tail. His jaw tightened. "They are."

She nodded as if she'd expected that. And likely she had. Damn it. He was tired of this. He wanted his fifteen minutes of fame to be over. He'd wanted it to be over three years ago when Rita died. So when he saw the main entrance to the rodeo grounds, he felt better. But not much. Damn snakes would probably follow him there, too.

"Did you know," she said as they pulled between the white fences surrounding the rodeo grounds, "that scientists fear belching cows are a major cause in ozone depletion?"

"What?"

"Scientists are worried about cow burps."

"You're kidding?"

She shook her head. "Cows expel between two hundred and four hundred quarts of methane per day."

"I had no idea."

"Neither did I," she said, then lapsed into silence. Chase wondered what other bits of knowledge her brain would spit up next, and how odd it was that she knew things like this.

No, not odd. Endearing.

"So if we have another ice age, you might be partly responsible."

And out of the blue, he smiled. Just as quickly he killed it, reminding himself he had no reason to smile. "Add it to the list of things I'm responsible for."

She glanced at him sharply, but he ignored her. Up ahead on the left, bleachers rose like a ghost town, empty now, but they'd be full to capacity come Friday night. The arena lay in front of it, chutes on the opposite side, with catwalks above. He supplied just the bulls for this particular rodeo. Another contractor would supply the broncs and event stock. When he pulled to a stop by the back pens, two other big rigs were already unloading.

Ah, hell. Every stock contractor, hired hand and rodeo official seemed to be there.

"Quite a party."

He nodded.

She moved, craning her head to see if the news van had followed. Chase looked, too. They had.

He jumped out. Maybe it was the tension he'd suffered during the ride up. Maybe he'd just had enough, but Chase was at the door of the pursuing van before the driver had time to react.

"Get the hell out of here."

The driver, a kid by the looks of it, leaned away from the window as if expecting Chase to smash it in. Chase felt tempted.

"Chase, don't!"

"Do you hear me?" he asked the kid. "Get."

"Chase—"

"Lani," Chase said turning back to her, "if you don't get them to leave, I can't promise I won't take matters into my own hands."

"I'll handle it," she said.

He stared from the van to Lani, knowing he truly was close to losing it. The events of last night, combined with this morning, and his pseudo-celebrity were all coming down on his head suddenly and undeniably. He left her to do her job while he got back in and reversed his big rig, nestling the end up against a delivery chute. But his head wasn't in the rodeo. He kept glancing over at Lani, hardly paying attention as he rolled up the truck's rear door. The bulls, only too anxious to leave, piled out with a hoof-stomping clatter. She wasn't done talking to the journalist, he noticed, sliding between the rails of the fence to stand on the ramp of his trailer.

He forgot to slide the chute door closed, a critical part of the process.

Heavy hooves stepped on the bottom of the ramp.

"Chase," one of the other contractors yelled.

Chase looked down his trailer's ramp, down at the black bull who'd turned back instead of keeping with the rest of the herd. The bull was looking at the man who stood between him and his destination—the trailer.

Oh, shit.

He tried to dive out from between the wooden boards.

Too late.

"Chase," he heard someone scream. Lani, he thought.

The bull hit him full in the chest. The one bull he owned that had horns.

"No!" LANI WATCHED Chase slide down the back of the rig. The bull stabbed at him again. Someone threw a hat at the enraged animal. The bull backed down the ramp.

Chase just lay there.

"No!" she screamed again, running.

The bull started up the ramp again. Another hat caught its attention. This time when it backed down, someone herded it past the chute door and then closed it so it couldn't get at Chase.

Chase.

Don't let him be dead. Please don't let him be dead.

"Someone call 911."

Lani didn't know who said it. She didn't care.

"Can't breathe," she heard Chase gasp.

The man who'd closed the bull off reached Chase's side first. "Just hang in there, buddy," the cowboy said.

Blood covered the front of his shirt.

"Oh, God, no." She didn't know she'd spoken the words aloud until Chase turned toward her, his eyes glazed with pain and something else. Fear.

"Chase," she said, climbing onto the ramp, clutching his hand, squeezing. "You're going to be fine."

"Can't...breathe."

"It's just the wind knocked out of you," the man on the other side of him said. "Just try to relax."

When the cowboy's gaze met her own, Lani could see the panic.

"Slow breaths, Chase. Slow," she encouraged.

Chase tried to move.

"No!" she and the other man both shouted at the same time.

When Chase's eyes closed, she knew he'd passed out.

"Jeez—" someone said, coming up behind Lani.

"Did someone call 911?" Lani asked, clutching at Chase's hands, watching the jagged rise and fall of his chest and praying it didn't stop.

And with every fiber of her being, she waited to hear sirens.

THEY'D HAD TO airlift him.

Punctured lung, she'd heard the paramedic say.

BP's too low for that to be the only injury, she'd heard someone else say.

But it was the way the two paramedics had looked him over, then looked at each other that had panicked her. They quickly called for the helicopter.

She didn't have a car. One of the other contractors gave her a ride. Lani hardly gave him a glance, just flung open his truck door and tried not to cry.

He'd been blue.

It was just the punctured lung. That was it, she tried to tell herself.

Why hadn't he regained consciousness?

They'd fix him, she reassured herself. They had to, because if they didn't…

No.

Lani had no recollection of the drive; she only knew she headed for a cardiac trauma unit nearly an hour away.

Why a cardiac unit?

He'd been blue.

When she jumped out of the truck, she realized every man at the rodeo grounds had followed, too. Lani ignored them all, turning toward the hospital's sliding glass doors, sickened by the antiseptic smell of disinfectant coupled with floor polish and people.

"My…" *lover, client* "…friend was just airlifted here," she said at the information desk.

"ER's through there," a gray-haired woman replied, pointing.

Lani raced to find someone in charge who could explain what was happening.

They'd taken him to surgery, and the look in the doctor's eyes who'd told her that, the way he tried to lay a reassuring arm on her shoulder—as if that would help—made Lani want to cry.

"It's serious," he said, giving her arm a squeeze.

"How serious?"

"They were giving him CPR when he arrived."

"No, damn it," she heard one of Chase's friends say behind her.

"Are you all family?" the doctor asked.

"Damn right we are," another man said.

"Then you can all wait over there." He pointed to a waiting area that Lani had barely registered. She was going to cry. She could feel the pressure of her sobs in her chest.

Chase.

"Thank you," she said in a small voice, having to take breath after breath to keep from breaking down.

He'd been blue.

"C'mon," said a burly man Lani vaguely recognized as the one who'd given her the ride. She stared up at him, trying to understand what he wanted her to do.

Don't let him die.

By then, her vision had begun to blur. She felt her fingers dig into her palms.

"I—" *don't know what I'll do if he dies* "—think I'm going to be sick."

"C'mon," he said again, using his big hand to guide her to a chair in the reception area. Lani stared at all the people around her. They all wore cowboy hats. Chase's friends.

"Miss Williams, can you tell me Chase's condition?"

Lani turned.

The kid from the news van looked at her from behind his camera, the light blasting her with its brightness.

"Oh no," she said, reaching up and covering the lens with her hand, her tears turning to rage. "Get out."

"Hey," the reporter said, pulling back. "Don't touch my camera."

"I'll touch a lot more than that if you don't get out," said someone behind her.

"I'm not going anywhere."

"Do as the lady says," the stout cowboy snarled.

"Yeah," said someone else.

The kid must not have been as dumb as he looked. He backed off. But Lani knew it was only a matter of time. Within hours, this place would be buzzing with press.

Chase.

She didn't care. She just didn't want Chase to die.

Chapter Seventeen

"We almost lost him," Dr. Steve Martinsun, the cardiac surgeon, told her. "He was in full cardiac arrest when he arrived. You're lucky the emergency personal transported him here. We're the only cardiac unit within two hundred miles and I doubt a local hospital would have recognized what was wrong with him."

Lani covered her mouth with a shaking hand.

"The rib that punctured his lung nicked a ventricle. The blood from the cut pooled around his heart, creating so much pressure the heart went into arrest, but once we opened up his pericardium he started to improve. We ended up doing a pericardiectomy. Took out just under a cup of blood. The release of pressure allowed the heart to function again and his vital signs to improve."

"Is he going to be okay?" Lani asked.

"His chances for recovery are good, barring any secondary problems. We're keeping him sedated right now because he's in a lot of pain. Had to crack open more ribs to do the surgery, but if he makes it through the next few hours, I suspect he'll be fine."

"Thank you," she said, feeling tears of relief flood her eyes.

"We're not out of the woods yet, Miss Williams. I'd like to see him stable for at least a few more hours. Let's just wait and see."

Lani nodded. The doctor walked away, his blue paper shoes crinkling against the white linoleum. The big cowboy she now knew as Jim put his arm around her shoulders. He led her to the same chair as before and helped her sit.

"Chase'll pull through," the man said. Some of the others gathered nodded. Young and old, short and tall, they all had the same expression on their face—fear tinged with discomfort as they tried to appear supportive.

"I've seen Chase get bucked off so bad I would'a sworn he was dead. Today was nothin'."

He'd almost died. Blood around his heart. If there hadn't been a cardiac trauma unit nearby...

"Kinda ironic, though, that Chase would end

up with the same type of injury that took Buck's life," one of the others said.

"He quit riding right after that accident." Lani didn't know the man who said that.

He'd almost died.

"Yeah, but he didn't quit because his traveling partner died, he quit because of—"

Everyone dropped into silence, the kind of quiet that precedes a comment when someone thinks he shouldn't have said something.

Rita.

Lani knew that's what he'd been about to say. And he had stopped because of her, because he thought she was now Chase's girlfriend. Except she wasn't so certain she was. She didn't know what she was.

"So, how'd you meet Chase?" one of the older men asked in an obvious attempt to change the subject. Stock contractor. She noted the name of his rodeo company on the pocket of his shirt. Chase had had his name on the front of his shirt, too.

Before they'd cut it off.

Before they'd shocked him to get his heart going.

Chase.

She took a deep breath, trying not to cry as she said. "I'm his press agent."

"You're a press agent?" someone else said, his surprise evident.

"I am," she answered absently.

"You been working together long?"

She shook her head.

"Well I'm glad he has someone to help him through the mess he found himself in," Jim said.

But, see, he may not need her help anymore. He may not even make it through the night.

Dear God, what if he didn't make it?

IT WAS A long day. Lani had called Amanda, and when Chase's friend showed up, her worried smile of understanding was all Lani needed to break down. Every man in the room looked away.

"Have you seen him yet?" Amanda asked.

Lani wiped her eyes and shook her head. "He's still in recovery."

"How long has it been?"

"Hours," Lani said, trying to stop the flow of tears.

"He'll be all right."

"That's what the goof troops have been telling me."

Amanda followed her gaze, a small smile flicking the edges of her mouth as she observed the lobby full of cowboys.

"I think every man from the rodeo is here."

"You're probably right. Rodeo's a tight-knit community."

"Where's Scott?" Lani asked.

"Talking to the press."

Lani glanced through the sliding doors. Sure enough, she could see Amanda's husband in front of a crowd of TV cameras.

"I would never, ever have thought that one little song could generate so much interest in a person."

"They'd be inside the ER if hospital security hadn't told them they had to stay outside—"

"Miss Williams?"

Lani turned. It was a different doctor this time. "I'm Dr. Edward Potter, chief of cardiology. I understand you're part of Mr. Cavenaugh's family."

"Yes," she said, trying without success to read the expression on the man's face.

"Would you like to talk somewhere private?" he asked with a pointed glance at Amanda.

Just tell me how he is.

"No," she said, her mouth dry. "She's family, too."

The man nodded, putting his hands in the pockets of his white coat. "His vital signs have remained steady for the past couple of hours. I don't see any reason why that would change. The anesthesia made him a little sick, but that'll pass soon. We're moving him to a private room within the hour."

Lani began to cry all over again, only this time it was in the shelter of Amanda's arms.

IT FELT AS IF an elephant had landed on him. Chase groaned in pain.

"Relax, Mr. Cavenaugh, it'll be all right."

Someone patted his arm. It was a nurse, he realized. The steady *beep-beep-beep* of a heart monitor told him he was in a hospital. He turned his head. Lani sat by his side.

"Hey there, cowboy," she said softly.

He blinked. Scott and Amanda stood behind her.

"Feel—"

"Horrible," the nurse finished for him, checking something on his IV. "Try not to talk, it won't hurt as much."

He hated hospitals. They were bad. Very bad. He looked over at Amanda. "Long?" he asked.

"Hours," she said, understanding his question.

Hours. The last thing her remembered was that bull—

Lani.

Pain.

"You were lucky," the nurse said. "Not many people get run down by bulls and live to talk about it.

Buck hadn't.

He closed his eyes; he didn't want to think about his friend now.

"That's it, folks," the nurse said. "Let him get his rest."

Lani squeezed his hand. He didn't squeeze back.

He heard Amanda come forward and he opened his eyes. As she leaned over him to give him a kiss, he whispered into her ear, "Send her home."

Amanda drew back, eyes wide. "Chase," she whispered back, "she's been here from the start. I can't just send her—"

"Home," he repeated, closing his eyes.

He didn't want Lani around. Didn't want her to see him like this.

Didn't want her to see his fear.

"HE WANTS ME to *leave?*"

Amanda glanced up and down the hall of the Intensive Care Unit.

"I'm sorry, Lani," she said, "but at this point, it's probably best not to get him agitated."

Lani didn't know which hurt worse, that Amanda told her this or that the woman took Chase's side.

"Did he say why?"

Amanda shook her head. "But when it comes right down to it—" She clamped her lips together, as if she hesitated to finish her words. Finally she said, "You really haven't known each other that long."

Lani felt as if she'd been hit. She wasn't family. It hurt.

"Will you call me when I can come visit again?" she asked, trying to hold back tears she didn't want Amanda to see. If she cried, she'd give away how much she cared for Chase, something that seemed ridiculous given the short time they'd known each other, as Amanda had rightly pointed out.

"I'll let you know."

And with that there was nothing much more to say or do except…leave.

HE NEVER ASKED for her.

Lani stayed nearby, handling the press from a hotel room in Pineville. The public had done one of its mercurial mood swings to embrace "Chase the wounded," though with the recent slate of articles and news blurbs about his charitable good deeds, perhaps it was more than that. Letters arrived. Bag after bag of them.

And flowers.

Masses and masses of flowers. Just dealing with that was enough to keep her busy, but it was so hard to stay away from Chase. Harder still when one of the nurses told her he'd been released.

With Chase back at home, Lani went back to Los Molina. Amanda had invited her to stay, but Lani refused. She'd retrieved her car from Chase's ranch long ago, but when another week went by with no word, Lani decided she'd had enough.

He didn't want to see her. Well, that was fine, but he was going to tell her why—face-to-face.

THE ROADS LEADING to the ranch were familiar enough that she had no problem finding her way. His front gate—a new one, she noticed—looked odd without the news vans parked outside.

It was locked.

She stepped back and stared at the lock for a full ten seconds. He'd done it to keep the press out, she told herself, but she was still irritated enough that she considered using her rental car as a battering ram. Well, not really. She did rattle the thing, but the rivets held fast. Fine. She would walk.

Her heel broke twenty steps down the driveway, likely loosened during her parachute landing off the front gate. She didn't care. Her other foot got sore fast, her shoe too tight across the back of her heel, a problem she'd known about, but one she'd always managed to cope with—until now.

When she got within sight of Chase's ranch, sweaty, sore and furious, she prayed he'd be there. If he wasn't— Well, she didn't know what she would do.

Fortunately, his truck was in the shed.

"I don't know whether I should hug you or

hurt you," she said as she burst through the front door without knocking.

"What the—" He came half off the couch, only to sink back down with a wince.

She strode in front of him, holding one foot higher than the other so he didn't notice her broken heel, though why she should care about that, she didn't know.

He looked gray. Not pale. Not colorless. Gray. That set her back on her heel until she recalled how he'd completely ignored her for two weeks.

"No, no," she said. "Don't get up. I'm only the woman who slept with you one night, who cried over your broken body. The woman who worried for hours that you would die. Don't worry about getting up. Or calling. Or sending me a note."

"Lani, this isn't a good time—"

"When *is* a good time, Chase? After you're over your fear of dying? Or your fear of another woman seeing right through you?"

His expression clearly said, "What?" even if his lips didn't.

She narrowed her eyes. "I know you didn't quit the rodeo because of the accident with Rita. You quit because you lost your nerve."

Chapter Eighteen

Chase would have gotten up if his damn body hadn't betrayed him. He would have told her to be quiet, too. That she had it all wrong. But he couldn't get a word in edgewise.

"She knew you'd lost your nerve," Lani said, hands on her hips as she stood in front of him. "That's what you and Rita were fighting about the night of the wreck. Yeah, that's right, Amanda told me she'd seen the two of you yelling, not when you were trying to get her in the car, but earlier, way earlier. At the rodeo."

"Lani—" damn, it hurt to talk "—not now—"

She flamed with righteous indignation as she stared down at him. "Then *when,* Chase? When you've come up with more reasons to push me away? When you've formulated yet another excuse for not letting a woman close to your heart?"

"What the hell are you talking about?"

She pushed his coffee table out, then sat on it even though it groaned in protest.

"I've been researching you, Chase. I know about Buck."

He rested his head against the back of the couch.

"I saw the accident he had with that bull. It was on a tape. *Bulls and Blood.* It showed you, too, that night, standing there by the chute Buck had just left from. They had a shot of the expression on your face while they were working on him."

"Lani, I didn't call you because I wanted to get better first."

"Bull," she said, her green eyes bright with anger. "You didn't call me for the same reason you shut yourself off from everything else. Fear."

She leaned even closer. "You used the accident as an excuse, let people assume you quit bull riding because of what happened to Rita. And everyone bought it, too. Poor Chase, they probably said, first his traveling partner, then his girlfriend. But you wanted everyone to think that, otherwise they'd question your decision."

Chase shook his head, telling himself not to react to her words. It wasn't good for him to get upset. "You've got it wrong—"

She got up abruptly. "I have it on tape."

Ridiculous. She'd gone off the deep end. Spurned woman. He should have expected this.

"I've watched them at least fifty times."

"What the heck are you talking about?"

"The two rodeos you competed in after Buck died."

He shook his head, telling himself his sudden anxiety had to do with facing an outraged woman. Every man feared that.

"You didn't qualify for the short go at either, something everyone conveniently forgot in the wake of the two accidents." She narrowed her eyes. "You were off your game, you told the media. Fighting the flu." She cocked a brow at him. "You lost your nerve."

"Look, Lani, I'm sorry for not calling you, but that's no reason for you to go hurling accusations—"

"What did Rita say to you the night of the accident? What was the *real* reason why you drank yourself under the table? Did she tell you to give it up? 'If your head's not in the game, you shouldn't be in the sport'?"

"Lani, you're meddling in stuff you don't know anything about."

She squatted next to him, her expression understanding. "I do know, Chase. You forget, I've been there."

Her friend. Her parents.

She grabbed his hand. "No one would have blamed you if you'd quit—"

"That's not how it was."

Her hand squeezed his. "No. You forced yourself to keep going, didn't you? Forced yourself to keep riding even though there was a good chance you might get hurt. Only it wasn't you who got hurt. It was Rita."

"Rita didn't die riding bulls."

"No, but she was afraid for *you*. She saw how you were riding, knew you were on edge. Except you told her not to be afraid, didn't you?"

How the hell did she know that—

"You told her you just needed to cowboy up or buck up, or whatever it is you fearless rodeo guys say to one another."

"I didn't—"

"And then she died," Lani said softly. "Died after being afraid to get in a car with you."

Chase couldn't move.

"And you felt responsible because you'd told her not to be afraid…afraid like you."

That did it. "Lani, if all you're here to do is nag me about my past—"

"Nagging? Is that what you think this is?" She got to her feet again, her face angry. "Is there a phrase book you men use when it comes to dealing with women? Under the heading of 'caring female,' does it tell you to call her a nag?"

"Obviously I'm not the only man to have called you that."

He could see he'd pushed her too far. The concern evaporated from her eyes. "No. Obviously you're not." And her expression clearly said, "Jerk."

Maybe he was. "Lani, listen, I didn't mean—"

"No, *you* listen," she said, stabbing her finger at him. "You have a problem, I know you do, and it's not just because of what happened when we made love."

When they…what?

"Or didn't you think I'd notice that you never…that you didn't…?"

"Unbelievable," he muttered.

"You're afraid. Afraid of letting yourself go, of feeling again—of what you might see in yourself if you do," she said in a low voice. "A coward."

"I'm not a coward."

"A cowboy's worst fear," she added as if he hadn't spoken, "is losing his nerve. When Buck died you lost yours. It made you stop bull riding. That and only that."

"Not true."

"I pity you, Chase. In some ways I think it would have been better if you'd been driving. At least then you'd have had a *real* reason to quit riding—you'd have been in jail."

The words stung. He supposed she'd meant them to.

"But tell me something," she said, straightening. "What worries you more about getting involved with me? That I'll die like Rita and Buck did, or that you'll start wanting to live again?"

Ah, hell. "I'm living my life just fine."

She shook her head, a smirk lifting the corner of her mouth. "Keep telling yourself that, Chase. Just keep telling yourself that."

She turned.

"Where you going?"

"Back to New York."

That shocked him. "You're leaving?"

"I'm leaving."

"Why?"

"No," she called over her shoulder, "I don't owe you an explanation."

And it was those words more than any that caught him off guard.

She put her hand on the door, paused for a moment. He thought maybe she'd admit those words had been too harsh.

"Do me a favor, Chase. When I'm gone, think about what I've said."

Chapter Nineteen

Lani left without looking back. She was proud of that. Proud of the way she held her head high as she hobbled down his dirt path, and pushed on the white, wooden gate guarding the entrance to his front yard.

It didn't budge.

She released a hiss, her hands shaking as she tried to open the gate. But in the perverse way of the world, the thing stopped working right at the moment she most wanted to make an exit.

She rattled the wood, her eyes filling with tears of frustration—that was what it was—frustration, not heartache.

"Come on, you darn thing."

Was he watching? Would he come out after her?

The latch gave. She pushed it open with more force than necessary.

He didn't come after her.

Well fine, she thought. *Let him sit on that chair and rot.*

He didn't even call out her name.

Well, of course not. She was a nag. All women were. At least, that's what Eric had proclaimed. And now Chase. Chase had called her that, too.

She sniffed, realizing that she'd lost the battle not to cry. Oh, darn it all anyway, why *not* cry her heart out? She'd just done her best to make the man see reason and he'd tossed it back in her face.

Called her a nag.

She inhaled a jagged breath, her lips starting to tremble.

He didn't come after her.

And that was the worst of it. Sure, he was injured. Sure, he might not be able to get up off that damn couch. But he could have called her name.

"SO YOU LET her go."

Chase stiffened, winced, the broom all but falling from his grasp as pain radiated down his arm.

"You let her just fly off without even saying goodbye."

The barn light framed Amanda Beringer's lithe frame. He'd been expecting her for the past couple days. Her hair was in its usual ponytail, but the black boots, jeans and shirt she wore looked like she meant business.

"We said our piece." He went back to sweeping.

"She said you were too afraid to let her into your life. Is there any truth to her words?"

Chase closed his eyes. Why did women need to meddle? "Amanda, I don't want to talk about it."

"Well *I* do."

The words shot like bullets off the walls of the barn's walls. Chase straightened.

"For years, Chase, three years, you've been handing me that line. 'I don't want to talk about it.' Well, I'm here to tell you, we're talking about it."

"Fine," he said. "Let's talk."

Amanda's jaw stuck out, something he knew from their childhood meant she was going to be stubborn.

"She told me I have a fear of dying."

Amanda's brows rose. He could tell Lani hadn't told her that part.

"That when Buck died it messed me up. She's wrong."

But she didn't look amused or surprised—or even disbelieving. She looked thoughtful.

"So that *is* what you and Rita were arguing about that night."

Chase jerked upright, even though it pulled on his wound. "Not you, too."

"It all fits."

"Lani tried to psychoanalyze me. Don't you try it."

"No, Chase, I think she was trying to help you."

He shook his head. "I don't need help. And I'm not afraid of dying."

He was afraid of failing.

"That's good because you'll need to be alive to go after her."

"I'm not going after her."

The rodeo was the only thing he had ever been good at, and that had fallen apart. His relationship with Rita had taken a hit. And before that, his parents.

"You better go after her, Chase, because she's the best thing that ever happened to you."

He was afraid of failing.

"Where are you going?" Amanda said as he dropped the broom and walked out of the barn.

"I don't know," he said. "Got some thinking to do."

"About what?"

About Lani, he silently answered.

THE SONG. The bloody, darn song.

Lani jerked on the knob of her office radio, the sound of Chase's voice something she couldn't tolerate, even after all this time.

Then why do you listen to a country station?

Because I like the music.

Why do you torture yourself by pausing every time a song starts? Wondering if it's "I Close My Eyes"?

She crossed to her window, looking out over the New York landscape. Gray buildings, crowded streets that looked yellow from this high up, thanks to the steady stream of cabs and masses of people who streamed along like ant trails. It was lunchtime. The ants were really marching now. Hurrah. Hurrah.

She stepped back from the glass, telling herself the dismal mood she was in was caused by the overcast fall weather. And even though it'd only been a week since she left, she missed the clear blue skies, open fields and—

Chase.

No she did not, she sternly told herself. She

most certainly did not miss that messed up, igno-
rant, ridiculous man. It was just hard not to think
about him since she still officially represented
him and now a new song had been released from
his CD. "Little Brown Bottle," a hilarious tune
about the pitfalls of drinking. It had made Lani
smile the first time she'd heard it, even as it'd
made her grit her teeth.

"Miss Williams, you're not going to believe
who's here!"

Jane, Lani's assistant of three years, had come
flying into the office with her hair streaming behind her like flames. That was no exaggeration.
Jane's hair was a fiery, improbable red, the short
strands moussed into Statue of Liberty spikes.

"It's him," she said, the emphasis on *him*. "The
rock star!"

For a second, Lani had no idea what she was
talking about. She didn't represent any rock stars.
Chase was as close to a rock—

She took a step back. "Mr. Cavenaugh?"

"In the flesh," said a deep, masculine voice.

Lani lurched back.

That was really a stupid thing to do, she
thought, as her butt bumped into the window. The
cold pane of glass made her instantly aware that

she wore a tiny black skirt and a thin white shirt. Her matching black jacket was slung over the back of her office chair, hanging there, empty arms sagging as if in disappointment. Suddenly, she lamented she wasn't wearing that jacket.

"Thanks, Jane. Would you please take Mr. Cavenaugh to the conference room?"

What is he doing here?

"That's okay," a masculine voice said. "I'm comfortable right here."

Lani stiffened.

Chase Cavenaugh—his ever-present cowboy hat didn't look at all out of place in the modern chrome-dominated office—stepped around Jane.

Jane looked from one to the other uncertainly. But the corporate world had taught her well. "Certainly, Mr. Cavenaugh."

"Jane," Lani growled, biting back her urge to scream, "don't you dare abandon me."

Instead she said, "Why don't you get us some water?"

"Sure, Miss Williams." But her assistant gave Chase one last my-my-my look before leaving him standing by the door.

"Have a seat, Mr. Cavenaugh."

He looked New York, Lani noted, in a cowboy

way. Black hat, black jeans and shirt. She would bet her female co-workers had all but drooled as he walked past their offices. One thing about Chase Cavenaugh, he looked good in his cowboy gear.

When she realized he was staring at her, too— no, when she realized that he realized *she* was staring at *him*—she blushed.

"What can I do for you, Mr. Cavenaugh?"

His eyes flicked over her, and for a second she had a feeling he might say something, something that would set her heart beating and make her heart melt.

But that was weakness on her part. She would not forgive him so easily for not calling her. Weeks. He hadn't picked up a phone and dialed her number in *weeks*.

And so she watched as he moved toward her desk, but he didn't take a seat. "I'm here to be on TALK! The television show with the tag line Hard-hitting Subjects, Hard-hitting Truths."

"You decided to do the show?"

He dipped his chin in acknowledgement. "I have. Your reasons for my making an appearance were good ones."

Yeah, but she hadn't expected him to actually do it. If she'd known he might come to New York…

You'd have what?

Made sure I wore loose clothes and pinned my hair back tightly.

"You look good."

"Thanks," she said, heading for her chair. The last time she'd worn heels around him, one of them had broken and she'd been forced to walk the long, long way back to her car.

Crying.

She sat. "Well, Chase, thank you for stopping by. It's good to see you. Please leave the name of your hotel with Jane on your way out so I know where to reach you—"

He moved toward her desk. Granted, she had a pretty big desk. Solid, white oak. But, she reminded herself, this was a man who dealt with fifteen-hundred-pound bulls when he wasn't crooning to the masses.

"I need your help," he said.

She kept her gaze even as she said, "Mariah is handling most of your publicity now. I only oversee it. Do you want me to see if she's available?"

"I want you."

Why oh why did those words make it hard to breathe?

He didn't mean it that way.

"Mariah is more than capable—"

"I want *you*."

"Mr. Cavenaugh."

Lani almost groaned as Mr. Abernathy entered her office, his gray suit matching his slick gray hair. The big cheese.

The big jerk.

He smiled like a used car salesman who'd just seen his biggest customer walk through the door. "I'm so glad you managed to make it."

Lani squinted.

"Thanks for making all my travel arrangements," Chase said.

Thanks for—

"Was she surprised?" Mr. Abernathy said with a wink in her direction.

Chase looked at her, a wicked grin on his face. "Oh, I guess you could say she was surprised."

Why that no-good… He'd *planned* this. With her boss's help?

She shot Chase a glare, but her anger turned to confusion when Mr. Abernathy said, "I took the liberty of clearing your schedule, Lani, so you can devote your time to Mr. Cavenaugh."

Lani's jaw dropped like a broken hatch. She

quickly snapped her mouth shut—years of training in keeping her expression neutral.

"Thank you," she said in a cool and professional voice.

"So what are you two going to do today?" Mr. Abernathy asked.

Lani knew she wouldn't like what Chase said, knew it with a gut-turning spasm. Her hands played with a pencil on her desk.

"We're going shopping," he said.

The pencil snapped.

SHE WAS FURIOUS. Chase had known she would be.

He'd come anyway.

He'd told himself to stay away. Told himself that if she was in love with him, as Amanda claimed, it was best to keep his distance. He was damaged goods. He knew that now. Thanks to her.

"Where do you want to go?" she asked as they pushed through a revolving door and out onto the crowded street. "Fifth Avenue?"

He shrugged, trying to stay as close to the building as possible so he wouldn't get jostled by the crowd. "Is it always like this?"

"Crowded? Yes," she said. "Limo yours?"

He nodded. The black Cadillac wasn't as long as some he'd rented in California, but it still got looks from the people passing by. Lani navigated the crowd like a cutting horse worked a herd of cattle.

"Well?" she asked as she climbed inside. She slid around the L-shaped seat so that she sat with her back to the driver, as far away from him as possible, Chase noticed. He stayed by the door.

"I need something to wear on the show tomorrow."

That wasn't strictly a lie. He really wasn't sure what to wear.

"Fine," she said, calling an address to the driver.

He took his hat off and ran his hand through his hair. He wanted to talk to her, but he wasn't at all sure what he wanted to say. Funny, 'cause he'd stared into the eyes of bulls. Ridden all sorts of rank animals. Faced off against the toughest cowboys in the industry. But suddenly he felt as scared as he had at his first Little Britches rodeo.

"Lani, I—"

"I don't want to talk about it, Chase."

Good. He didn't either. Except he had to. He owed her that much.

"I was a jerk."

She looked at him with the stern expression of a teacher who'd lost her patience with a student. "I said I don't want to talk about it. It's ancient history. You and I are over. Not that we ever got off to much of a start."

He stared at her, horns blaring outside as the limo navigated the stop-and-go traffic. This wasn't going the way he'd planned. Hell, nothing had gone right since she left. The press still pursued him. His song was still on the charts. Now, a new song had been released, and his lawyers were unable to do a thing about it other than file more motions. No number of threats had convinced the big label that now owned the rights to his songs to stop releasing them. They had an ironclad contract.

"How have you been?" he asked.

"Fine," she clipped out like a single shot from a six-shooter.

"I'm sorry I didn't call."

She shrugged. "No big deal."

"I was mad," he said.

"So was I." She glared at him, obviously still angry.

"I was wrong."

Her eyes narrowed, her jaw tight, before she looked away. Chase admired the perfect shape of her profile, her blacker-than-black long hair. And the realization clicked inside him then—these thoughts would have scared the hell out of him two months ago.

"I'm sorry, Lani."

"Yeah, well, so was I." But she still wouldn't look at him. The gray light inside the limo made her skin look even paler than normal.

"Forgive me?"

"No."

He laughed. It hurt his broken rib. Hell, his whole body still ached. "Let me buy you dinner?"

"The cows in your pastures will sprout helicopter blades before I go out to dinner with you."

He chuckled. "I'd be disappointed if you agreed easily."

Her eyes narrowed, and he could tell she was weighing her words, testing out one or two in her mind. "You hurt me."

"I know," he said back. "And I'm sorry." He truly was.

She looked away again.

"Just dinner," he said. "I owe you that much."

She began to shake her head.

"Please," he said, sliding along the seat until he was close enough to reach out and take her hand. She had nowhere to go, no place to move, but her body language all but darted off the seat.

"If you don't say yes, I'll have to get Mr. Abernathy to make you go with me."

She tried to tug her hand away. "You wouldn't dare."

He stared at her pretty face, at the familiar eyes that touched him with their honesty. "Actually, I think I would."

MISERABLE JERK of a man, Lani thought as she waited in her apartment lobby for Chase's limo four hours later. How dare he? she thought as she adjusted the thin straps of her black dress. How dare he ask her out? How dare he pretend that nothing had happened between them? All day long he'd been courteous—

Sweet.

Fine. He'd been sweet to her. But she wasn't buying it. No way. No how.

It was good to see him.

No. It. Was. Not.

He looked good. *Healed.*

Who cared?

That's what she told herself. Heck, she wasn't going to have her head turned just because he'd tried to buy her a watch, and a new dress he'd claimed matched her eyes.

She was not.

When the limo arrived, she didn't wait for Chase or the driver to open the door. She just darted out of her building, opened the darn door and slid inside.

No Chase.

Lani stiffened.

The limo driver gave her a wry look in the rearview mirror.

"Where is he?" she asked.

"Mr. Cavenaugh made dinner arrangements at his hotel."

She sank back against the leather seat. So he was going to get her to eat at The Plaza after all. Well, bully for him. She would still be just as cold, just as polite as she had been all afternoon. He would learn that he couldn't order her around.

But the concierge who came out to greet her didn't lead her to The Plaza's four-star restaurant. He led her past the reception desk, through the grandiose lobby with its large chandelier, red carpet and mirrors, directly to a set of elevators.

"Where are you taking me?"

"I was ordered to deliver you upstairs."

His room? Oh, no. No, no, no.

The floor he pressed was one story up. Her brows lifted in confusion.

"Where are we going?" she asked as the elevator doors opened.

"This way, ma'am."

The hallway was decorated with more white crown molding, red carpet and lavish flowers arranged in stands between several ballrooms. They stopped before one of those ballroom doors.

"I don't under—"

"Your corsage," the man said, handing her a clear plastic container with three, perfect roses inside, which had been hidden behind a potted palm.

"My corsage—"

He opened the doors.

Lani gasped. She covered her mouth. The corsage fell to the floor.

Oh, God.

Balloons floated above the tables. A banner hanging from the ceiling said Stars For A Night.

It was a prom. Chase had turned one of The

Plaza's ballrooms into a replica of a traditional school graduation party, complete with a four-piece band on a dais at the end of the room.

"You said you never got to dance at your prom," a masculine voice said from behind her. "I thought you deserved at least one dance."

Oh, Chase.

He stood, an expression on his face that was part tenderness, part concern, part hope.

"I don't know what to say."

He came toward her, his black tux—the old-fashioned kind with bow tie and black cummerbund—taut around masculine arms. No cowboy hat.

"I do," he said softly, his hand reaching out to cup her face.

Lani swallowed a lump in her throat the size of the silly disco ball that spun over the dance floor. "You once told me there are no do-overs in life." He smiled tenderly. "But you're wrong, Lani. There are some things we *can* do over again."

She didn't even care that tears had begun to fall down her cheeks.

"You can dance at a prom."

She blinked, more tears falling.

"You can dance with me."

She was shaking.

"You can give us another chance."

She forgot to breathe.

"Will you, Lani?"

There are no do-overs.

Her words came back to haunt her. Dare she do this over?

Yes, whispered a voice, one that sounded like her childhood friend, Esther.

She took his hand.

Chapter Twenty

It was the most magical night of Lani's life. They'd danced and talked and learned more about each other in one night than most couples likely learn in a year. She told him about her mother, and how she used to sing so well Lani had believed her mom when she'd claimed to be one of the vocalists on the radio. It was only later in life when Lani had realized the truth—had laughed with her mom about it.

He told her about his life as a teen, about the trouble he'd been in and out of. How he'd discovered the rodeo when he was in high school and never looked back.

And when later, he invited her up to his room, Lani went with him. It was hard to say who felt more nervous, her or Chase. But this time, when Chase brought her to the summit of pleasure, he followed her there, Lani holding his hand.

And crying.

She realized that she was in love with him that night. Had been in love with him when she'd left Los Molina all those days ago.

When she woke up the next morning, he was gone. Lani felt a stab of mortification followed by fear.

Not again!

He'd left her a note this time.

Lani,

 I don't want you to think I'm running off. I'm not. I have to do that damn talk show...

The talk show. She'd forgotten.

 You looked so peaceful this morning, I didn't have the heart to wake you.

She smiled.

 After the talk show I need to take care of something, something I have to do on my own. The room is paid for. Stay as long as you like. I'll call you.

He'd *call* her?

And what did he mean he had something to do? *What?* And why didn't he tell her face-to-face? What was going on?

A glance at the clock revealed that he'd already taped the show. And that she was late for work.

Damn. She'd call in sick. Everyone in her office would know that was a clanker, but she didn't care. Nor did she care that she used office personnel to track down Chase's whereabouts.

No go.

Nobody knew where he was, not even her boss.

"HE'S IN OKLAHOMA CITY," Amanda's voice came over the phone.

Lani sank to her couch. He'd been missing for a day. Lani had been about ready to fill out a missing person's report.

"What's he doing in Oklahoma City?"

"He's entered in a bull-riding competition."

"In a *what?*"

"Scott's arranged for one of Global Dynamics' jets to pick you up at La Guardia in an hour. The event starts at seven. Depending on when he rides, you might be able to catch him beforehand. To stop him, Lani, it's too soon for him to ride. We'll meet you there."

Lani slammed the phone down and packed a bag, her hands shaking.

Bull-riding! What was he thinking? The man still hadn't recovered from his injury. She'd touched the scars Thursday night. Lani shook her head. Getting back on, hurting himself again… The weak rib might nick his ventricle again, and this time it might be fatal.

HER HEART WAS in her throat when she arrived at Oklahoma City's Ford Center dome. The indoor sports complex was the largest in the state, and Lani realized too late that finding Amanda in such a mass of people would be next to impossible. The event had already started, and the man at the ticket office explained that they'd been bucking for almost an hour.

Chase.

She ran down the near-deserted corridors, listening to the roar of the crowd inside. But then the roar turned to a groan as if someone had gotten hurt. Or fallen off.

Chase.

She burst out of the narrow tunnel that led to

the arena with enough speed she mowed down a yellow-coated security guard.

"Whoa there, lady," the black man said.

"Has he ridden yet?" she asked, suspecting she might look a bit deranged.

"Who?" he asked.

"Chase Cavenaugh."

"Who's that?"

"The singer, Chase Cavenaugh. He's riding a bull tonight."

The man nodded, his face shiny from the fluorescent lights. "Oh. That guy," he said. "Hasn't gone yet as far as I know."

Lani wanted to clutch the man's burly shoulders in relief. She hadn't missed him.

"But we're almost done."

She straightened abruptly. The security guy pointed to the arena, which seemed far, far away from where they stood.

"How do I get behind the chutes?" Lani asked.

The security guy laughed. "You don't. Not without a pass."

But a quick scan of the arena revealed that she could get close, if she traveled to the left.

"Thanks," she said, turning away.

"Faster to use the elevators to get to the main floor," the man said.

But she wasn't going that way. She was going to try and call out to him. Once she got his attention, she knew he'd wave her through, and then she'd read him the riot act. What the heck did he think he was doing?

It's his turn to have a do-over, Lani.

He had no business doing *this* particular thing over again, especially right after his injury. This was dangerous.

It's something he feels he has to do.

She understood that, but, she reasoned, there were other ways he could accomplish the same thing, such as riding back at home, on a bull that was a little tamer.

What would be the point of that?

Chase needed to face his fear head-on. He couldn't do-over the moment Rita had died, but he could do this. Ride the bulls.

She burst into the main arena, this time careful to slow down before she hit another security guy. But now that she was here, her confidence faltered.

What the heck was she doing?

Lani looked around the stadium at the hundreds of fans that watched the chutes. She knew why they were so fascinated. People didn't watch bull-riding to see cowboys ride, they came to watch them fall off. To get hurt.

Then she saw him. Chase's back was to her, his beige safety vest proclaiming just how dangerous a sport this could be.

Chase, she silently called out.

She couldn't move.

He needed to do this, she realized, tears in her eyes. Damn it. He needed to do this without her distracting him. Without her interference.

CHASE SAT SLOWLY on Undertaker. The bull felt his weight and tossed his head.

"You sure you're up for this, buddy?" Tim asked over the noise of the crowd.

Chase nodded, concentrating too hard to form a reply.

Takes a jump out. Turns right. Likes to spin low. May change directions. Don't get caught off guard.

"He's a nasty one," Tim said.

Chase started to pull his bull rope taut. Tim took up the slack, helping him pull. Undertaker snorted in rage. Chase's gloved hand rubbed the rope, heating the rosin, making it sticky, tacky, easier to grip.

"Good," he said.

Tim let go. Chase grabbed the loose end of the rope and laid it against his right hand, palm up against the bull's back.

There are no do-overs.

Lani's voice came back to him, and for a moment he hesitated. But just for a moment.

Focus.

He tugged and wrapped, careful to get the rope nice and tight. Undertaker blew up when the loose end flicked him.

Bam.

The sound echoed down the other chutes. His knee against the wooden gate. Pain. In his chest. In his leg. He grit his teeth.

I'm too old for this.

He felt the bull start to go down. Someone slapped him. Up he went, his head twisting in rage. Chase's knees tightened. More pain.

And then came the moment of stillness as bull and rider gathered energy. The silence of a rocket about to be launched.

Chase nodded.

The gate swung open.

Undertaker grunted.

They went up. This time there was no gate in the way. They hung in the air.

Center. Stay centered.

Thump-thump, thump-thump, thump-thump.

His heart. It was all he heard. Not the crowd. Not the announcer. Not the music.

Undertaker came down, and Chase rocked back. They turned. Chase's inside leg tightened.

Ignore the pain.

Thump-thump, thump-thump, thump-thump.

The bull's tail slapped him. He ignored the sting against his cheek.

Breathe.

Chase sucked in a breath. So did the bull, the snort filled with anger. Up they went.

Two seconds? Three?

Three seconds. Five more to go.

He's turning.

Chase felt his weight shift.

Tighten. Shift. Stay centered.

His arm muscles strained.

Hold on.

The ground grew near.

Undertaker paused, turned…in the other direction.

What?

Hang on!

Chase's vision blurred. Moisture hit him. His sweat? The bull's?

Five seconds.

Up they went again. He couldn't hold it. It was too much. He was too old.

Six seconds.

His weight slid to the left. *No.*

"Son of a—" Blood filled his mouth. Chase bit down harder.

Seven seconds.

"Not today—" *You don't have me today.*

Eight seconds.

Brrrrrrrrrr.

Chase heard the buzzer and let go.

But his hand stayed in.

No.

His weight tipped.

No.

His body slid. But his hand was stuck.

He was hung up.

"Get 'im, get 'im," one of the bull fighters shouted. Someone screamed. Odd how Chase could hear that single cry.

Two-thousand pounds of infuriated bull bumped into him.

Not good. In a moment Undertaker would see—

The bull turned his head.

Uh-oh.

Dusty, the rodeo clown, jumped into the arena, distracting Undertaker from Chase.

Chase tugged and his hand came free.

The crowd screamed. The bull charged the other man, and Chase ran for the arena chutes. His ribs ached with each breath, his arm searing from the abuse. He climbed just as his decoy darted out of the bull's path. Someone opened a gate. Undertaker turned, paused, his sides heaving, then trotted out as if he hadn't just tried to kill a cowboy.

"Way to go," Dusty said after the dust settled, handing Chase his bull rope.

Chase's smile lit his face. He hadn't felt like this—well—since Rita had died. "Dustin, if you weren't so darn ugly, I'd kiss you for saving my behind."

"Shoot, Chase, tease me why not?" the clown said, slapping him on the back.

The crowd erupted. It took Chase a moment to realize why.

Ninety-two.

He'd won the event. And if Chase had been the kind of cowboy to cry, he would have cried then. Hell, his eyes stung anyway.

He'd done it.

I wish Lani could see this.

Every man, woman and child was standing. He gave them a wave.

I should have told her.

He turned back to the chutes.

And that's when he saw her. She stood near the rail to the right of the chutes, her hands clenching the banister as if it would save her life.

Chase froze.

Slowly, ever so slowly, she straightened. Even from this distance, he could see the tears sparkling in her green eyes. Her hands came together and she clapped. Clapped and smiled and cried—and before Chase realized what he was doing, he held out his arms.

She needed no second urging to climb the rail like any true cowgirl would do. It was a good five feet to the bottom of the arena. Chase caught her as she jumped.

"Lani," he said, his world feeling right.

"Chase," he heard her say, her voice choked. He saw tears falling down her face as she looked up at him.

"I did it," he said to her.

"You did it."

"I rode Undertaker."

She began to smile. And then laugh. "That bull's name is Undertaker?"

He nodded. And then he smiled, too. His head dipped down and he kissed her.

The crowd went wild.

"I came here to stop you," she said after pulling back.

He stilled. "Why didn't you?"

She grew still, too, the whole arena watching as Lani stared up at him.

"This was something you needed to do. I may not have liked it, but I had no business stopping you. You are who you are, Chase." She took a deep breath before saying, "And I love you."

Her bull-riding cowboy placed his hand against her cheek as he said, "I love you, too."

Thirty-thousand people were watching.

Lani took a deep breath.

"Go. The network is waiting for you."

He glanced over at the TV crew standing near the chutes, looking back at her with a wry grin. "Ever the PR agent."

"Actually, I would rather keep you to myself."

"So would I." He glanced at the newscaster assigned to the event. "But I'll make you a deal. You go over there with me. Stand by my side, and I promise you can have me to yourself for the rest of our lives."

Lani felt her breath catch, had to stare into his eyes for long seconds to make sure she understood him.

"Will you marry me, Lani?" he asked. "I can't promise it'll be easy, but I can promise you'll have this cowboy's heart forever."

Lani let the tears come in sobs. She didn't care if she looked like a fool. Or if TV cameras were recording her blotchy face and red eyes. She just didn't care.

"Oh, Chase," she said, hugging him, bumping his hat off his head. They laughed as they scrambled to pick it up. But when she tried to say the word *yes* she could only stare at him and cry.

Chase Cavenaugh, the man who'd spent the past few years holding in his feelings, also had tears in his eyes.

"I take it that's a yes?" he asked.

She smiled up at him. "Well, I don't know," she teased. "You know that fifty percent of marriages end in divorce."

"Don't tell me you're going to say no because of some trivia you learned for a game show?"

She laughed. "Why would I let that happen," she said, "when the other fifty percent last a lifetime?"

He smiled. "So is that a yes?"

It was her turn to place a hand against his cheek. "Yes," she said softly. "Oh, yes."

Epilogue

The rodeo had just begun. Mutton-busting, the first event, was underway. Tiny green panels held sheep nose-to-nose so kids could ride them. The sheep bleated in protest, rodeo personnel and parents standing nearby to help out. The grandstands were full to capacity.

Chase Cavenaugh paced, trying to calm himself as he inhaled the scent of kettle corn and hot dogs.

"Hold on tight," Lani was saying as she leaned over the tiny chute, a *sheep's baa-aa-aaa* momentarily drowning out her words. "Let go if you feel yourself start to fall off. Don't try to hang on."

"Mo-om," their five-year-old daughter said, her black pigtail hanging out from beneath her gray helmet. She rolled her green eyes as she met her father's gaze. "I've done this before."

Chase stopped pacing as Lani said, "Yes, but every time is different."

Rose released a breath in the exaggerated way kids had when they'd lost patience with their parents. "Daddy, she's making me nervous."

Chase looked at Lani. Lani gave him a petrified smile.

Chase couldn't help but laugh. "Lani, it's just a sheep. A little, bitty tiny sheep. Her feet just about drag on the ground." Never mind that he had just been pacing. That was different. Excitement. Yeah. He was excited for his daughter.

"She's only five," Lani said.

"I'm in kindergarten now," said Rose. "A big girl."

Chase suppressed his laugh this time. Headstrong, outspoken and far too much like him to suit him, Chase could do nothing but watch as his daughter did her best to imitate dear old dad. Oh, and the boys. It still boggled his mind that out of three children, neither son had any interest whatsoever in riding bulls. 'Course, one was less than a year old. And the other was three, but the three-year-old preferred to watch his little sister from the comfort of the stands with the Beringer boys.

"You ready to go?" one of the officials said, looking down at Rose.

Her eyes wide with excitement, she nodded.

"Open it up!"

"Careful!" Lani cried.

But her daughter was already gone. The sheep took off like a cat with a pack of dogs at its heels, Rose holding on like a tiny jockey.

Chase beamed with pride. Sure, her feet were dragging on the ground. Sure, she looked more like a circus monkey riding a dog. He didn't care. The crowd of family and friends who'd come out to watch the Los Molina Little Britches Rodeo clapped in approval as Rider 121 rode that sheep, number card flapping in the wind. A few minutes later, when the judges held up their chalkboards, they applauded even louder.

Eighty-six.

Not bad.

His daughter, showman that she was, waved her hand, after she'd dusted herself off, of course.

"Maybe by the time she makes it to college, she'll be able to ride with the men," Lani said.

His grin faded. He faced his wife and said, "Over my dead body."

Lani widened her eyes, pretending to be

shocked, when, in fact, they'd had this conversation before. "Chauvinist."

"You bet."

And though they stood at one end of the arena in plain sight of the spectators' stands, Chase leaned down and kissed her.

Lani closed her eyes. It never ceased to amaze her that every time her cowboy kissed her, she still felt the same jolt she had the first time their lips touched.

Charlie, the man up in the announcer's stand, must have been watching, or maybe it was just good timing, but a familiar song began to play over the PA.

"You Filled My Heart."

"Your song," Chase murmured.

"Our song," Lani corrected, the one he'd written for her, the one that had stayed number one for almost eight weeks. But it wasn't Chase singing it, it was George Strait, which always made Lani feel a little odd. She remembered the first time Chase had strummed his guitar for her, the first time he'd looked into her eyes and sung the words.

You filled my heart. And made it whole. And I thank my lucky stars. You filled my heart.

Tears came to her eyes as she leaned forward and kissed him again.

"Dad-dy," came their daughter's voice.

Lani and Chase looked down at Rose.

"Yuck," she said, shaking her head in exasperation.

Chase smiled, and leaned forward to kiss Lani again.

You filled my heart, Chase thought. They'd filled *each other's* hearts.

"Would you two stop it?" Rose hissed.

Chase drew back and stared down at his wife. "Not in this lifetime."

Lani smiled. Not in this lifetime.